DETECTIVE TRIGGER
AND THE RUBY COLLAR

BOOK ONE

M.A. OWENS

For my wife, who said:

"You should write a book about [our dog] Trigger, as a private detective."

And, at long last, here we are.

ACKNOWLEDGMENTS

Carissa, for giving me invaluable advice on my plot and characters.

Eric, for his fantastic editing, allowing so many things I was struggling with to finally fall neatly into place.

Dani, for beta reading and being a constant source of encouragement.

Les, for her masterful graphics design, turning my illustrations into jaw-dropping covers.

A special thanks to Jagal, my illustrator, who has been such a pleasure to work with, and who has gone so far above and beyond for every piece of art I've commissioned. For reading my books, and genuinely caring about the characters and the story. If anyone reading this ever needs an illustrator: jagal.weebly.com

GET THE PREQUEL FOR FREE!

If you finish this book, and find yourself wanting more, I've got you covered. For the most enjoyment, finish reading *The Ruby Collar* first!

MAOwens.com/FREE

1

Arc City. Home to countless flea-bitten scoundrels looking for as little trouble for themselves as possible. As for the rest of us, though, we expect nothing but trouble. I keep a low profile these days, sticking to the easy money cases. I was just a small-timer, and in more ways than one. Being a little brown Chihuahua put me at a big disadvantage to even the cats around here. And me being a one-eyed private eye didn't do me any favors either. I was the private detective you'd expect to hire at a dime-store discount. Along with the propaganda-filled morning newspaper, I had the pleasure of reading yet another "Your Bill is Overdue" love letter from my dear old landlord. As I was sitting at my desk contemplating my financial burdens, a sudden knock at my office door startled me.

I cleared my throat. "Come in."

Let me tell you, this dame was a looker. A white coat with a few spots here and there, she was a Chihuahua like me, but with a long, thin face and a tail that curled just a little on the end. She had large black eyes that matched her pricey black dress. She was the kind of dog you'd see in the papers in one of those big-dollar ads trying to sell me expensive junk.

"Are you Trigger?"

"I am. What seems to be the trouble, ma'am?" I asked.

She fumbled with her kerchief, dabbing her eyes before she spoke.

"Oh, sir, it's just awful." She stopped to sob, sniffing loudly and wiping her eyes again. "Dreadful. You see, my most valuable possession has been stolen."

"What did the cops say?"

"I came to you first. You have a reputation for getting a job done quickly and with results."

I looked around the office. Cluttered. Things knocked over and never picked up again. Dust so thick it could've been a coat of paint on half the room. This dame didn't fit well in that picture, and I could tell she wasn't giving it to me straight.

"Didn't go to the cops, eh?" I grunted.

"No, sir. See, this isn't just any collar. It's covered with fine red rubies and what's more, you see... well, there just isn't another like it in the whole world. It was my mother's. And it was all she left to me."

I looked down at the bill on my desk for a long while as I thought about the fifty different ways this kind of case could go south. Pretty dame. Expensive heirloom. Goodness knows who she's going to say stole—

"Mr. Trigger? Are you interested in taking this case?"

"I haven't said I'm not."

"I'm prepared to offer you five hundred dollars for—"

I shot up from my chair as if someone just lit up one of the old newspapers on the floor. After all, if they did, the whole place would go up in about a minute flat.

"That's a month's salary for a lot of dogs. No one offers that kind of dough on a small job unless the pooch they're offering it to is about a week away from turning up in the Arc River with a brand-new pair of concrete slippers sized just for him."

"Mr. Trigger, I assure you you're in no significant danger. The criminal who I believe stole it is very elusive, but he has never been known to be violent."

I sat back down in my chair, producing a shrill squeak from wheels that had gone too long without a good oiling. In actuality, I was just putting on a show and would take the case no matter what. Five hundred dollars would keep the lights on for months. My options were either get killed on the job or starve to death. Some cases are lousy enough to make even that choice tough. At least this case could be a bit more exciting. Makes it easier for a dog to gamble big when he's got nothing to lose.

"So, who do you think has it?"

"Rico, the master thief. I'm sure you've seen all the stories about him in the newspaper."

"Rico, eh? Lady, no one's laid eyes on that pooch in years. Almost every cop from one side of this city to the other would give his left paw to be the one that brought him in."

"You don't think you could find him?" she asked.

"I might be able to find him. How much are you paying up front?"

"I'll pay fifty up front."

"Ha! Lady, I'll take two hundred up front. And that's being generous."

"I'll give you a hundred."

I stood up and held out my paw. "You've hired yourself a private detective, Miss...?"

She offered her paw in return. "Lily. My name is Lily."

2

I snooped around the usual places. Museums. High-dollar jewelry stores. Wherever I could think of with merchandise worth a lot of dough. I also spent the day interviewing several of Rico's previous victims. I was just going through the motions. Nobody figured out a way to predict Rico's next heist, so it all came down to luck. He didn't make the usual mistakes. He left no obvious clues. He never got carried away on sprees nor did he taunt the police. He went long periods of time without stealing anything, and he hurt no one while doing it. A real professional. At least the easy hundred would keep food on the table for a while.

Everybody's always afraid to talk in this city, worried they're being sized up by one of Mr. B's goons with some kind of trick question. Can't blame them for thinking that. That's usually what it is. He sends lackeys around and they play like they're some kind of a private eye like me - just to see what they know about this or that crime. Next thing they know they're getting roughed up, or worse. Can't say I'd do a lot of talking either if I was in their shoes.

I kept up this routine for about a week. Friday morning, I put the key in my office door and realized it was already unlocked. I pushed it open to find a dog that wasn't me sitting in my chair. He was a beagle with a black mask and a silly bandit costume you'd expect to see in a low budget film. I knew who it was the moment I laid eyes on him.

"You looking to hire a private detective?" he said.

"A real wise guy, aren't you?"

"Oh, lighten up, Trigger. Learn to laugh a little. Smile."

"You come all the way here to give me comedic advice?"

"Well, it sounds like you could use it. But no, I didn't. Word gets around fast in this city when a dog goes asking questions."

"Never heard of any words causing anyone harm, Rico. You could've just stayed in that hole you were hiding in. We both know I'd never find you."

"Well, that may be, but I'm taking an interest in this case of yours."

"You should find it interesting. You're the one who stole the collar I'm supposed to find, after all."

His eyes brightened up, and he smiled from ear to ear.

"Sure, I've got it. I'm thinking I might even give it back to you too. What do you think?"

"I think you have an angle. There's something in it for you. So why don't you just get on with it and spit it out, Rico."

"What if I said I was looking to hire a private detective myself?"

"I'd say you probably give the best comedy advice around, a guy as funny as you."

"Comedy routine's over, Trigger. I can go get that necklace for you. You just can't tell that dame how you got it. As for what I want, there'll be five large for you when we're done. Interested?"

"That's the kind of cash you get offered for a suicide mission, if you're fool enough to take it. Get out," I demanded.

"Come on, you don't even want to he—"

"I said get out!"

He frowned a big fake frown when I pointed to the door. But just as he stood up to leave there was a knock.

"If you change your mind and want to hear more, tie a black ribbon to your trash can out front," he whispered. And without another sound, he escaped through the back door.

"Come in," I called out.

It was Lily again. Who else? If only she'd come a few minutes later or earlier, things might have been a lot more interesting.

"Mr. Trigger. I don't mean to trouble you, but have you any news of my mother's collar?"

"Not yet, ma'am. I've still got a few leads so don't go giving up hope just yet."

She reached into her purse and pulled out a hundred-dollar bill, handing it over.

"I'm sure this has taken up a dreadful amount of your time, detective. I want to make sure all of your expenses are being taken care of, so consider this advance a token of my gratitude."

I took the bill and nodded.

"You're being awfully generous, Ms. Lily. Any occasion for such a thing?"

"No occasion, detective. I'll leave you to your work."

She turned and walked out. Now things were getting interesting, but interesting is just the thing a dog wants to avoid if he wants to live a long life. Do-good types didn't exactly have a lot to look forward to in Arc City.

I reasoned through it in my head. Rico figuring out I was looking for him; that was easy. Rico coming to me and floating a five-thousand-dollar job... that's a little tougher. Lily coming to me and wanting me to find a valuable ruby collar; sure, I get that. But why did the dame come back and offer another hundred after holding out on me the other day? I had a feeling I would regret it, but I only knew one way to put it all together.

That night, I tied a piece of black silk to the handle on my trash can out front.

3

Monday morning came and I headed into my office early. Sure enough, the scoundrel was sitting right there in my chair again.

"Looking to hire a private detective, sir?" he said.

"This routine again?"

"Eventually you'll find it funny, detective. You just need to relax a little. Have a nice strip of bacon sometime. Tastes even better when someone else paid for it."

"I didn't think you were the type to steal anything that wasn't top-shelf merchandise. Have jobs gotten a bit slow these days for the master thief?"

"I was just suggesting you could buy me breakfast next time, detective. You invited me over, remember?"

"You sure like small talk, don't you?"

"Don't you?" he said.

"Small talk is for dogs who don't have cases to solve. I invited you back because curiosity got the better of me. By the way, why did you come back? You know I could've had the cops stake this place out and pick you up. Make a big name for myself."

"No cops were staking the place out."

"I said I could have done it."

"You wouldn't."

"You seem awful certain of that."

"Certainty is my trade."

The big grin on that smug face of his really bristled the hair on my neck. He was right. I didn't have much tolerance for criminals, but in this city, sometimes you have to choose the lesser of two evils, and that's precisely what I did when it came to Rico.

"You know me awfully well by the sound of it. Humor me. Why wouldn't I do it?"

"You don't get along so well with the cops in this city from what I hear. I heard you were a police detective some time back."

"Easy now." I pointed my paw right at his face, the hair down my back standing on end.

"From what I also hear, that didn't turn out so well for you. Sound about right?"

I slapped the papers off the desk in front of him. They scattered around the room and further littered the already cluttered floor.

He grinned as big as he could manage. "You need to do something about that temper of yours. You asked, remember? Maybe you wouldn't be so sensitive about your past if you did a few more things you could be proud of. And speaking of doing something you'd be proud of..." He crossed his arms and leaned forward on my desk, a serious expression washing over his snide grin. He motioned for me to lean in, so I did. "How would you like to take down Mr. B and his gang? That ought to help you sleep at night."

I felt my stomach twist at the mere thought. I stood back up slowly.

"See, now you're back in your comedy routine. The only ones who get a good night's sleep in this city are the dead, and the fastest way to join them is to go stepping on Mr. B's toes. You must have lost your mind, or do you have some kind of death wish? What kind of fool messes around with Mr. B, huh? And why?"

"You're talkative all of a sudden."

"Well, you certainly know how to liven up a conversation. You done kidding around now? You ready to tell me what you really want?"

"No more jokes, detective. You're a smart dog. Tell me what all my thefts have had in common. Surely you've figured it out by now."

"Yeah, I figured it out a long time ago. So what?"

"Out with it then," he said.

"Everything you swiped was from an establishment either owned by Mr. B's gang or working with it. I assume Mr. B was always quiet about it to avoid the embarrassment, so nobody ever pieced it together. So what?"

"You know what," Rico said. "Aren't you tired of living in a city run by thugs? A city where dogs and cats just trying to get by get bullied by Mr. B's goons and can't live peaceful lives? A city where crime pays and no good deed goes unpunished?"

"I manage just fine. I keep my nose clean and help

just enough not to get noticed by any big players, at least until now."

"Is that really good enough, though? Doing just enough not to get noticed? You haven't done something right in this world if you haven't made any enemies."

Rico really knew how to kick a dog where it hurt. I couldn't argue with a thing he said. Here I was getting lectured about having guts and doing "the right thing" by none other than a wanted criminal. It used to be me talking about the same thing, but time had turned me into a coward.

"Sleep on it. All I'm asking is for you to hear me out. I'll be back to see you soon."

4

I picked up the paper the next morning. There were the usual crime sprees, most of which were in the Black District where I called home; the poorest part of the city. One particularly nasty story was about a grocer who got his store smashed up. His whole life savings gone in a single night. Poor cat's got a family too. Should've picked another place to settle down, I guess. I'm not even sure why I read the paper anymore. Mr. B pretty much owns that too. I read the interview.

"Mr. Clive, can you tell us what happened?"

"You can see what happened. Everything in the whole place is destroyed."

"Sounds like you upset the wrong people, Mr. Clive."

"Yeah, I upset the wrong people. I quit the gang. Me and Lucy. We left the scene about a year back."

"While we don't condone crime here at the Arc Daily, it sounds like you knew what you were getting yourself into and you took your chances."

"You're right. This was my fault."

What a load of garbage! There's no way he said that last line. I wadded that paper up in a fit of rage and hurled it against the wall. Crooked cops, crooked newspapers, crooked journalists. Rico was right. What's it all for if you sit around day after day and do the same thing you've always done, drinking the same cup of joe while sitting down and reading the same paper? They print the same hooey on it every day. For me, I sit in this chair and wait for somebody to come in with something easy - something that's not going to upset anybody. Some dame misplaces her earrings and thinks someone robbed her. Some dog wants to check up on his pup who didn't come home last night. Easy stuff.

I go home, sit down, and eat the same dinner. I watch the same stupid shows on the picture box, and used to listen to that made-up detective show on the radio. The one about a real detective who solved big cases. That was before they had it taken off the air. Then I go to bed and toss and turn half the night, barely getting a wink of sleep. I do the same doggone thing over again the next day.

All the while, the city gets turned upside down and pockets get turned inside out. I watch like it's all just another show on the picture box. Occasionally, I'd get a little glimmer of courage in my heart and I'd lie to myself, "Tomorrow. Tomorrow I'll change things." Only, tomorrow never came, because tomorrow always turned into today.

I grabbed my hat off the rack and flipped the sign to "Out to Lunch." I headed straight down to that grocer's place. It was not all that far away. I started asking questions of the neighbors and other business owners. Folks were afraid to answer, like always, but I finally loosened enough lips to find out where the grocer lived. It was late, but I headed there to have a chat. His house was just a few minutes' walk away from his store.

I knocked and a kitten answered the door.

I tipped my hat. "Your mom or dad home, missy?"

A feline dame came running toward the door. "Clive, you're finally home!"

She stopped and looked at me with disappointment as she got close enough to realize I wasn't who she thought I was.

"Your husband out, ma'am?"

"Who are you?"

"Trigger, ma'am. I'm a private detective," I said, tipping my hat.

"Why do you want to see my husband?"

"I've taken an interest in your family's troubles. I read about it in the paper, and I didn't buy that phony interview for a second."

"Heh. It's a phony all right, a real hit job. I warned him not to talk to them, but he wanted to get the truth out. Wanted to let everyone know what he thought of that cutthroat Mr. B. I heard him too. Let them have it. The fool."

"Your husband. He out?"

"He went out to survey the store and see what he could salvage. He wants to start it back up again. Got more guts than brains, I'll tell ya."

"Thank you for your time, ma'am. I'll head back that

way and see if I run into him." I tipped my hat again before turning to leave.

"You don't think he's in danger, do you?" she asked.

I shook my head. "I'm sure he has a lot to look over. I wouldn't worry too much."

I smiled, turned around, and kept walking. My pace quickened after I made it out of sight of the house. You work in the business long enough and you get an intuition for this sort of thing. He was definitely in danger.

5

I was about to round the corner at the grocer when I heard a commotion. Glass breaking. Hollering and hissing. I peeked around the corner. Several big cats, nearly twice my size. They were rough characters to boot, surely Mr. B's goons. Looks like they came back to finish the job.

No doubt Mr. Clive was inside. He probably hid out when he saw them walking up. I had to think of something quick. I walked a few buildings over and yelled, "Mr. Clive, where are you running off to in such a hurry!?" I darted down an alleyway and hid behind a dumpster, peeking out to watch the street. Sure enough, the guys I saw took off down the road after the imaginary Mr. Clive. Too easy.

I circled back around and ran into the store, looking in every possible hiding place I could think of. I had to be quiet. If I yelled out again, they might hear me and come back. I opened one cabinet behind the cash register, and then out hopped a scared cat swinging a piece of broken glass at me as he went for the kill.

"Easy, Clive. I'm not one of Mr. B's goons."

I dodged the first strike, and then he stopped dead in his tracks.

"Mister, I don't know who you are, but I'm glad you came when you did. Sorry about swingin' at you."

"Don't worry about it. I sent those thugs on a wild goose chase, but they'll be back soon enough. We gotta move it."

We ran out the back and hoofed it back to his house. The cover of night made the whole thing a lot easier. Few people to see and ask questions and go ratting us out. Lucy met us at the door, running out and hugging Clive as we ran in. The little kitten ran out and clutched onto his leg.

"Oh, Clive, you made it. I've been up waiting, worried sick! Little Darla, too." she said.

"It's all right, Lucy. I'm fine now. Go wait inside and let me talk to my friend here," Clive said.

She placed her paws onto the kitten's shoulders, leading her back inside. Then she turned to me. "Thank you, detective. I won't forget it. What do we owe you? I'll fetch my purse."

"No charge, ma'am. This one's on the house."

She took the kitten into the house and closed the door.

Clive turned to me and put on a tired face.

"You think they'll give up, detective? You think they'll let me be?"

"You want the straight answer, kid, or the one that'll let you sleep good tonight?"

"That's all the answer I need. I thought as much," he said.

"Can you leave the district in the next few days? Take your family and get out of here? You can lie low in the Capitol District for a while."

He frowned. "No can do, detective. For one, I'm not running... and even if I wanted to, everything I had was tied up into the store. I bet it all. Insurance in this city won't cover Mr. B and his gang no more. I won't see a dime from them."

"You call the cops?"

"Yeah, they said they'd look into it."

Just hearing those words made me grind my teeth. "Oh, yeah. I'm sure they'll look into it. Looking is probably about all they'll do. They do a lot of just looking, so I'm sure they'll do a fine job at it. Best to have a report on file though, just in case we ever get a chief that's not bought and paid for."

"Are you..." He looked at the ground, going quiet.

"Am I what?"

"Are you going to get in Mr. B's way, detective?"

"You don't need to concern yourself with my job, kid. But let's say a dog would make trouble for Mr. B. Would you help that dog out?"

"I would."

"You've got it bad enough already. Think it over. Carefully. Things are bound to get a lot worse for you as time goes on. Talk it over with the wife."

"I got a family to take care of, detective. I want Darla to grow up in a city where she doesn't have to look over her shoulder everywhere she goes, where she don't get dragged into a life of crime like I did. Crime's been in my family for years, Detective. I want to get it out. I want to get it out of the whole rotten city."

I smiled. It was looking more and more like I wasn't the only one feeling that way. "Better lock those doors tonight. Come by to see me tomorrow and make sure you're not followed. My office is just twenty minutes down the street. You know the place?"

"You're Trigger, aren't you?"

"That's right. You heard of me?"

"Yeah, but I didn't really know who you were. I sure know who you are now, though."

That moment I felt like I could relate to that big-shot detective that used to be on the radio. I felt like maybe I could be the hero on my own radio show someday. I might even make it into one of those crazy detective novels. It felt good.

6

I opened another letter the next morning. "Final Notice" was stamped across the top. I frowned and tossed it on the desk when a knock came at the door.

"Come in."

It was Clive.

"Were you followed?" I asked.

"No, sir. I left early and took the long way around. Made several stops along the way, just like you told me."

"Have a seat." I pointed my paw to the chair in front of me. "So, tell me what it was like on Mr. B's crew? How did that start?"

"Well, my mom and dad died when I was just a kitten. I never found out how. They just never came home one day. So I lived in the alleys and went digging around in the trash for scraps. Eventually I found a few other kittens do the same and we sort of formed our own little crew, you know?"

I nodded. "Sorry about your parents, kid. Go on."

"We didn't really make much trouble. We'd steal

sometimes, sure, but we only stole food. If we had something we didn't need, we'd try to leave something in its place, you know? We weren't bad kids. Not really. But we all gotta eat, know what I mean?"

There was a time more than a few generations ago where dogs had the run of the city. Cats weren't allowed to own businesses, vote in elections, or even be cops. They mainly lived outside the city walls, but I'd never been outside the city. I couldn't say what it was like. Few knew what it looked like outside the city, much less what it was like to live there.

I'd lived in the Black District long enough that I'd seen kittens like Clive running around looking for scraps, fighting just to get the next meal. I've met a few pups like that, too. Dames would have more pups and kittens than they could take care of by themselves, then mommy and daddy get desperate trying to bring home the bacon. They'd get mixed up with the wrong folks, then, sure as the summer rains, something would happen to your dear old parents and... Boom! You get strays like Clive. I'd probably seen Clive at some point, too. Wish now I'd paid more attention to some of their faces since most of them end up getting recruited by Mr. B.

He noticed me getting lost in thought and stopped talking, tilting his head in concern. I motioned for him to continue.

"One day, when we were a little older, I was out with my boys. We messed up bad. There was two cats talking outside a restaurant we liked to hang around. Big shots in suits. We could tell they were scoping somebody. They were trying to blend in, but we could tell they weren't from our hood. They didn't really know how to blend in. They were too focused on this one table outside. Probably had a meeting scheduled. Say, detective..."

"Yeah?"

"You gonna write any of this down?"

I pointed to my head. "Yeah, in here."

"This seems like an awful lot for you to keep straight in your head."

"Let's say someone followed you and you didn't know it. Let's say I get Mr. B's attention some other way. You believe they should come in here and find written testimony from you?"

"You must have a good memory."

"A little too good. There's plenty I wish I could forget," I said, dropping the matter. "Anyway, the big shots."

"Oh, right. So, this one big shot had his wallet bulging right out of his coat pocket. The thing was so full of cash it was about to burst. See, we'd never stolen money before, but money buys food. So, well, we came up with a little plan to nab the wallet. One of the boys came over and said he was the son of the restaurant owner. He wanted to know why they were snooping around. Another one came down the street about that time and threatened the one pretending to be the owner's son. Saying he had beef with him. They made it real convincing. Scrapped right in front of these guys. Claws out, that kind of stuff. Blood and all."

"You really went all out on the distraction," I commented.

He nodded. "These guys didn't want the attention and tried to break up the fight. I was hiding nearby. When they were good and caught up in what was happening, I snuck right up behind them and pulled the wallet right out of his pocket. Then I took off. I ran all the way back to our usual meeting spot. The other boys didn't break character either. They were calling names and making threats all the way down the street. Could've been actors on the television.

"So, we finally get back to the meeting place and this wallet... well, sir, it really was full to bursting. We're talking about a grand or more. We should've been terrified to see that much money, but all we could think about was all the food that money could buy. We rented ourselves a nice little apartment to stay in, we went out and bought some nice clothes, went to some nice restaurants. That's when everything changed."

7

"Dramatic. How did everything change?"

"That's where I met Lucy."

"Lucy. The mother of that little kitten I saw last night?" I asked. His face lit up brightly.

"That's right. That's Lucy. She was working at one of the fancier joints in town, waiting tables. I never had the confidence to talk to a dame like her before, no sir, but it became a lot easier now that I had some nice clothes and some money in my pocket. I asked her to go to the movies with me and she agreed. Me and Lucy dated for months. Got to be inseparable.

"One day, we were all at the apartment having a meeting when a knock came at the door. Several big cats greeted us when we opened it. All dressed sharp, like the two we lifted the wallet from at the restaurant. There was no helping it. You don't turn down cats like that. They ask to come in, we let them in.

"These weren't just the muscle types, detective. A couple of these were cats used to handling a lot of dough.

Bean counters. They talked smooth. One says he liked what we did with the money we stole. Could've heard a pin drop in that room. We thought for sure we were done for, but they stayed cool. The muscle too. The other bean counter asked when we'd be able to pay them back in full, and what kind of interest we thought was fair. We were just some dumb kids. We didn't know how to talk money. We just knew how to spend it.

"Finally, one of our guys spoke up and laid it out for them. Said we would've loved to pay all that money back with interest, and that's the stone-cold truth. We weren't just saying that because we were scared. Well, it was because we were scared, but what I mean is we weren't lying. We meant it. Only we didn't have that money. They offered us a payment plan, saying we were lucky because their boss needed cats just like us to work for him. And he paid well.

"We all agreed to work for them. To take whatever jobs he needed us to do. Only he didn't pay so well like they claimed, and these jobs weren't the kind to make for a good night's sleep. We beat folks up, we robbed, we muscled cats and threatened dogs. We collected debts. Sometimes people ran. Sometimes they had the means to fight back and gave us a sound thrashing." He pointed to his leg. "Got this leg busted up bad when we went to this one Doberman's place. Charles was his name. Gave us all the beating we probably had coming. Two of the boys were pushing up daisies after that tango. He got a visit from the *real* muscle the next day, but that didn't bring our boys back, you know?

"Anywho, Lucy kept waiting those tables. Worked real

hard. I kept doing any job I got asked to do. I didn't buy nothing I didn't need to live. Stashed it all back. After a couple years of that, we finally had enough between the two of us to pay my share of the debt. I asked for a meeting with the bean counters and they agreed. I got invited over to one of the nicer locations. I put on my suit I'd got a couple years back. We treated it almost like a holiday, detective. All the other boys got sucked into the life, but all I ever thought about was getting out of it. It was all thanks to Lucy, you know? She kept me on the straight and narrow. She supported me. She knew I had to do some bad stuff, but she forgave me for it.

"So, I show up at this place, and everybody's real cordial. Real polite like. I get asked to come in and sit down. This older cat's sitting at a big desk in the back. Slickest dressed cat I ever seen. His watch probably cost more than the money I'd ever see in two lifetimes. I handed him the money, and he had one of his boys count it for him. They gave it back. Said there was a problem. He opened this big black book and ran his paw along the pages. Said I was way short. Most of the other boys didn't pay, and that meant I had to pay their share. I told him where he could stick that money I owed. I lost my cool and messed up, detective, but I was so mad. I worked hard and paid my whole share back. Plus the interest. On time. The other boys worked out their own deal and liked their new work.

"He warned me that nobody ever crossed Mr. B and lived peaceful afterward. I thought I was a dead cat for sure. For a while, we kept our heads low, nothing happened. That bean counter must've been trying to pocket money on the side by asking for more because if that came down from the top, I wouldn't have made it home that day. Talk about a stroke of luck.

"Me and Lucy started over. She got promoted to assistant manager at the restaurant and got me hired as a waiter. I worked hard. Always showed up on time. Always did my best. Finally, we saved up enough that I bought the old grocery store down the street. Mr. B's boys would come by occasionally to ask for more money. You know, for 'protection' and whatnot. I finally got to see what it was like to be on the other side of the baseball bat. I told them to get lost, and the interest grew more and more. Nobody could pay what they were asking. It was a real scam. You know the rest, detective. They stopped just asking, stopped threatening."

I nodded. "Does two hundred get you and your family out of this district for a while? Long enough for things to blow over."

"I don't take charity."

"I don't take advice on how to run my business from grocers, kid. I'm paying you for the information you gave me, and not even a good rate at that, but that's all I got to pay. Take it or leave it."

He looked down at his feet. After all that's happened, his pride must've shrunk to almost nothing.

"Okay, detective. I'll take it."

I handed it to him and he stood up.

"Thanks for everything. I won't forget it." He didn't wait for me to answer. He hung his head and walked out of the room in a hurry.

I looked down at the "Final Notice" letter again and

shook my head. There went my rent money right out the door. I couldn't seem to help myself. This big heart will be the death of me one day. I'd have to figure something else out or that day would come sooner than I'd like.

I tied a strand of black ribbon to the trash can.

8

The next day I headed to my office. It was unlocked, but it wasn't Rico in the chair this time. Instead, I had the building owner looking down at me. He was a pug named Charlie. Charlie used to be an architect some ways back. Wanted to go back to his neighborhood and design beautiful buildings. He was good at it, too. Seen some of his work when I first rented the building, plans hanging on the walls and a few sketches here and there. Too bad he didn't design this hole. Ended up getting no clients in this part of town and had to resort to renting his old office to bums like me.

"Mr. Trigger, I believe you know why I'm here," he said. I could hear the vitriol in his voice.

"Good to see you, Charlie. Can I get you something to drink?"

"Just water, please."

I poured us each a glass and sat down on the other side of the desk.

"Mr. Trigger, have you been getting your notices in

the mail?"

"I have."

"You realize that you're now two months behind on your rent?"

"I do."

"Trigger, when I rented this building out to you, I thought it would be easy money. I knew you had troubles in the past when you were a cop, but you had a reputation for having a very sharp mind. I believed you would solve big cases, one right after another while having clients lined up out the door. But what I really believed even more was that you were a pup who knew what terms like "late" and "past due" meant and that you understood the fact that when you stop paying your bills, you reap the consequences. So what happened?"

"I think you'd make a good private detective yourself, Charlie, with the way you sneak up on a dog like that and ask the hard questions."

"It's my building. One can hardly sneak into a place they own. Something that I can't say about you right now."

"Maybe I'm not the big-shot detective you thought I would be. Maybe you screwed up renting me this place from the start. Maybe you're not a great judge of character, Charlie," I said.

"You've got till the end of the month. Pack up your things and get out. I'm going to be finding another tenant as soon as possible. But, if by some miracle, you manage to get the money, you can pay me by the end of the week."

"You never know what could happen in a week."

Charlie nodded and frowned, then he got up and

walked out the door. I always felt bad for Charlie, but he felt bad for me too. Guess we both fell a little short on expectations. He didn't become a great architect, and it looked like I might not be a private detective for much longer. I got up and moved to my chair. I sat there looking at the notice for another couple of minutes, trying to convince myself it would all work out when I heard the door pop open on a small supply closet in the room's corner.

"Looking to hire a private detective?" Rico asked.

"That's real funny." I used the most sarcastic voice I could muster.

"You didn't tell me you would have a guest this morning."

"Wasn't expecting one."

"I gathered. So, you thought things over?"

"I have. I'll hear the rest of what you had to say about the case."

"Very generous of you, detective. May I have a seat?"

I nodded toward the seat in front of me. He smiled graciously and sat.

"What made you have a change of heart?"

"The grocer incident. You read about it in the paper?"

"I don't believe most of what I read in the paper, but yes I heard."

"I helped the cat escape a good thrashing at the hands of Mr. B's goons. I sent him on his way yesterday with a couple hundred bucks to get him and his family out of the district. I got testimony on how he recruits too."

"It doesn't seem like you have cash to give out, detective."

"I had it. Then I gave it out. Going to tell me the plan, Rico? Or we going to gab the whole morning away?"

"I need you to find out who Mr. B's biggest cat, or dog, is in Adria District and get close to them," Rico explained.

"Adria District? You mean the upscale place with all the museums and fancy restaurants? A lot of dough moves through there."

"That's right. You might remember, but a year back I picked off a couple of nice pieces from that art museum."

"I remember. I also remember the pieces just so happened to be owned by Mr. B. So, what do you need me for if you already know all the ins and outs?"

"I'm not in a position to go asking questions around the place. Those in the know are a little more difficult to buy off or win over," Rico said with a smirk.

"Think they're going to talk?" I asked.

"I think they will."

"I'm all ears."

"There will be a bit of a mishap soon. Some expensive items will go missing, or something to that effect."

"I bet I can guess who the saboteur will be."

"Bet you can't, detective." There was that sly grin of his again.

I nodded. "Glad you considered the problem in advance."

"They will have themselves a real genuine mystery on their hands. There'll be rumors going around about a certain private detective. With any luck, someone will come to see you. You'll be taking the case, getting in close, and doing your digging on the boss while solving it. Shouldn't be too hard for a hardened pooch like you."

"Sounds hazardous. Requiring a sizable advance."

"That'll be taken care of, detective. I'm prepared to give you a thousand up front, cash. Pay your rent and get this place cleaned up, would you? It's disgusting. I don't want these big shots walking into a dump, holding their nose, and walking right back out."

"You don't think it adds charm?" I laughed.

"Oh, it adds something. 'Charm' isn't it."

He retrieved an envelope from his vest pocket, tossing it onto the table in front of me. I took the money out and counted it. I paused and gave him a suspicious glance.

He gestured to the envelope and feigned distress. "You think I would cheat you, Trigger? You wound me."

"Where's the collar?"

"Oh, that thing? I didn't steal it. I knew you wouldn't believe me at the time if I said so."

I clenched my teeth.

"What? Believe it or not, I don't steal everything that gets stolen."

"All right, so now I have two cases to work on then. Guess I better get busy."

"Need a suit?"

"I got a couple of nice suits from when I was at the department. They don't suit me."

He grinned. "Now who's the comedian?"

I scoffed, giving him a sidelong glance before shaking my head. He reached out his paw, I reached out mine, and we shook.

"It's a deal then," he said.

"It's a deal."

9

He mentioned a mishap soon. That gave me some time to regroup about this collar business. While I waited for Lily to come back, there was the matter of shaping this place up.

I walked down to Charlie's place, letting him know I took on a new case and got a small advance. I paid the two months behind and for the current month. You should've seen the look on his face. Probably thought I was pulling his leg about not having the money when he came by.

I spent the next several hours cleaning up the office. Bag after bag of trash. Old papers. Food wrappers. You name it. I did some sweeping. Wiping down the walls. Moving furniture. Even did a little mopping.

The front lobby looked lonely now. I had a secretary a while back I had to let go when things got slow. I called her and asked her if she could come back. She was happy to oblige. Zelda was her name. A fine gal, but old as the hills. She mostly did the job to stave off the boredom of retirement after her husband passed.

She showed up within the hour.

"Good to see you again, Trigger," she said.

"You too, Zelda. Hope you didn't get too bored at home."

"I must have read about a hundred books, so it wasn't too bad."

"Must've spent a fortune on a hundred books," I replied with a sly grin.

"I reread the hundred books I already own."

I couldn't help but laugh. "Sounds like I called you just in time. You were losing your marbles."

She chuckled and went about setting up her desk.

The next morning Zelda buzzed into my office. Scared the daylights right out of me.

"There's a Ms. Lily here to see you, detective."

I pressed the button on the intercom. "Send her in."

She opened the door and walked inside, looking surprised, if not downright impressed.

"Mr. Trigger, I like what you've done with the place."

"Thanks." I motioned to the seat in front of me. "Please."

"I wanted to check in with you to see if perhaps you've discovered any new leads about my stolen collar."

"Hit a snag with that, ma'am. See, when I was on the force, I spent a lot of time studying Rico's markers. I went over all that in my head. This just doesn't fit the profile."

"What do you mean, detective?"

"I mean that I don't think Rico lifted your collar. A

collar is an easy thing to pocket. When was the last time you saw it?"

"It had been in the armoire for years. I would look at it every few months, just to clean and care for it. I rarely wore it." She paused. "I suppose I saw it about a month ago."

"Lot can happen in a month," I muttered. "Who had access to the room during that time?"

"My maid, but she's a darling. She'd never steal a thing. Not a thing."

Yeah, sure. "Anyone else?"

"Some members of my family and a few friends, but they don't really have a reason to enter the room."

"Does the room stay locked?"

"No, it doesn't."

"What's the maid's address?"

I slid her a pen and a pad of paper across the desk. She picked it up and wrote down the address.

"Afraid I will need to talk to her about it, ma'am. It's the best lead we've got at the moment."

She frowned. "If you must, detective, but please clarify that I don't suspect her. She's just such a dear. I'd hate ever so much for her to believe I think ill of her."

"Stop by whenever you want and check in, but I'll ring you up when I find out anything new."

"Thank you."

"Have a good day, Ms. Lily."

She stood and walked toward the door. "Take care, Mr. Trigger."

10

Grabbing my coat and hat from the hanger, I was ready to make my way toward the maid's place. She lived in one of the shadier parts of the district; that's a low bar already. She was a young cat, but I still gave the precinct a ring to check on any priors. Sure enough, she had a record. A domestic with a boyfriend about a year back, and a petty theft charge about a year before that. Lo and behold, I had myself a prime suspect. Could've turned out to be a straightforward case.

I walked down the street where she lived, taking in the surroundings. Everyone I passed gave me a nasty look. This was a cat neighborhood. They apparently didn't take kindly to a dog sniffing around where he didn't belong. Come to think of it, cats really used to get the short end of the stick. That's why Mr. B's somewhat of a folk hero to a lot of these kids, at least until they realize he'll use them and throw them away just as quick as he would any dog.

Once upon a time it was the dogs who ran this city.

Cats had their own city, if you could call it that, not far away; but it was always getting attacked. That led to an agreement of free movement between them and us. A few dogs went there. A lot of cats came here. It really threw things out of balance in the city. The skills the cats brought with them weren't much good here. A lot of dogs resented having a bunch of freeloaders coming in who only seemed to be interested in causing trouble. After just a few months, the free movement was limited to just those leaving the city, and no one was allowed in anymore. By then, though, the damage was done.

Most of these unfortunate travelers were easy targets for criminals looking to hire cheap muscle to get their point across. The dogs here didn't trust the new residents, so cats weren't allowed to join the police force, vote in elections, hold office, or own businesses. A lot of the cats did just fine. They found work and climbed their way up the ladder at some existing companies. The opposite type of cat settled in Black District. Things have changed a lot these days, but there's still a lot of resentment among the cats here. And that same resentment has been passed down through the generations. They just don't take kindly to dogs coming around.

I finally arrived at my destination: a small, cramped apartment. One of the nicer ones in the area, actually.

I knocked on the door.

A young male cat answered, looking me up and down. He poked his head out, looked side to side, and then behind me. His eyes darted about, looking out for who knows what.

"You a cop?"

"No, I'm not a cop. Is Molly here?"

"She in some kind of trouble?"

"No, she's not. I just need to ask her some questions."

He narrowed his eyes. "You sure you're not a cop?"

"Wouldn't I know it if I was a cop, kid?"

"You'd know it, but maybe you wouldn't want me to know it, Mister..."

"Name's Trigger. Going to get my name and not give me yours?"

"That's right," he said. "Besides, Molly ain't home."

A voice shrieked out from inside. "Robby, who's that at the door?"

Robby sighed and looked at me with a hateful scowl.

"Some dog here looking for you and asking a lot of questions. I was just about to give him what for."

"It's okay, Robby," she interrupted as she came to the door. "I'll talk to him."

Robby gave me one more heartfelt glare before disappearing into the apartment.

"Am I in some kind of trouble?" she asked.

"Should you be?"

"What do you want?"

"Lily hired me to look into something that's gone missing from her house. And—"

She looked at me like I just stepped on her tail. "And she thinks I stole it!"

"No, ma'am, she doesn't think you'd actually ever steal anything."

"And you?"

"Mind if I come in?"

She motioned for me to come inside. I took off my hat and coat, handing it to her. She looked uncomfortable by my doing so and showed reluctance in hanging it up for me, but she did anyways.

"Have a seat," she said.

I sat on the couch.

"What did you say your name was again?"

"Trigger, ma'am. I'm a private detective."

"Sorry I shouted at you. I was just surprised is all. Ask your questions."

"You ever been in trouble with the law, ma'am?"

"Not really."

"Can you be more specific?"

"Can you, sir?"

"No, ma'am. I mean just that. I'm asking if you've ever been in trouble with the law. A straight answer will make this go quicker and smoother for the both of us."

"Sure, I've been in trouble with the law, detective. Aren't all cats in some trouble at some point in their life?"

"What sort of trouble were you in?"

"I got jealous of my boyfriend talking to another feline and I didn't handle it very well."

"How did you handle it, ma'am?"

"I gave him a claw across the face. He called the cops."

"How long they put you up for that?"

"I just got slapped with community service."

I nodded, impressed. Our justice system at work. "Got off lucky, then. No more trouble with the law before or after that?"

"No, sir."

"You're sure about that?"

"I'm sure."

I looked down at my watch. "Are you sure, Molly? Maybe if I give you a minute or two to think about it you'll remember."

Her eyes go wide. "No. Robby!"

11

I turned around in time to see a broom handle coming square at me. I got careless, wasn't watching my six. I took a lick to the back of the head, and it staggered me for a not-so-brief moment. When I was finally able to come to, I grabbed the handle on the next swing. I wrestled with Robby on the hardwood floor while Molly screamed like a maniac. It was enough to make the kid lose his nerve and let go of the handle. I gave him a quick jab to the gut with the broom handle for good measure.

"Still think I'm a cop?"

He struggled to catch his breath. Not sure he would have said anything even if he could. He got to his feet after a moment, taking off out the door. Molly looked on, her paws covering her gaping mouth.

"You ready to give it to me straight now, ma'am?"

"I took some jewelry, all right? I took it. I have it all right here! Come and look!"

I cautiously followed her into her bedroom, awaiting another feeble ambush. She pulled out a brown box from underneath her bed. *Finally, we're getting somewhere.* I would be glad to get this case over with sooner than later. She took the lid off the box and I peered inside. There were two pairs of earrings and one small ring, but no collar.

"You sure this is all of it? You don't have more stashed away elsewhere?" I inquired.

"No, sir. This is all if it. You've gotta believe me. I want rid of it. Call the cops if you gotta."

I sighed. "I believe you, but I'll be taking this back with me. Hope you'll forgive the intrusion, ma'am." I turned and walked out the door with the box in tow after pulling my hat and coat off the rack.

I had only just stepped out the door when a sharp left hook caught me right in the jaw, forcing me to drop the box. On instinct, I countered with a left hook of my own that hit home, bringing this strange cat to his knees. I felt a sharp pain in my side as I took a kick to the ribs. This scrap got serious; I was in some real trouble. I snuck a quick glance over my shoulder. It was Robby behind me. Must've grabbed a pal.

I sank my teeth into Robby's shoulder, and he let out a terrible squall and swiped me good in the face with those claws out. Thankfully, on the already blind side. I knocked him to the floor and gave him a swift kick to the kisser. I snatched the jewelry quick as I could and sped off.

I ran as fast as my feet could carry me. Wobbled and staggered about like I was running in a strong wind. Just a couple of small-time cats roughed me up good. Talk about a blow to the ego. Maybe Rico was wrong. Maybe

I'd listened to too many detective shows on the radio. Maybe I was only cut out for the small times after all.

I finally made it back to the office, stumbling inside.

"Mr. Trigger!" Zelda jumped up from her desk.

"I'm all right. Tell anyone who calls or comes in that I'll be back tomorrow."

I retreated into my office and locked the door. I always got like this. I lost my nerve when things got tough. I had to get my head together. Dad always told me courage was the thing you do when you're just as scared as everyone else. He said you didn't have to take any steps forward. You just had to be willing not to take any steps back. Me? I found that courage was a muscle you train. You know when the right time is and you do it. Every time after gets just a little easier, but it never gets easy.

Man, this blow to the head would make for one whale of a bump. I looked down at the intercom, but my vision went blurry. I pressed the button, then blacked out.

12

I woke up to the sound of machines beeping. Zelda was sitting in the corner, a dog in a white coat stood over me.

"Mr. Trigger? Mr. Trigger? I think he's waking up," a voice declared.

I squinted and tried to sit up, only to have a pair of paws gently, yet forcefully push me back down.

"Mr. Trigger, you're in a hospital. You need to relax. Lie back."

"What's the damage, doc?" I asked.

"A slight concussion which caused some swelling. That's why you passed out. You've got lacerations—"

"Am I going to make it, doc?"

He sighed. "You'll make it, Mr. Trigger, but you need to take your injuries more seriously. The swelling isn't too bad and is going down nicely, but you'd be doing a favor for your life expectancy if you stay out of brawls. For a couple of weeks at the very least."

"Good, fetch my papers so I can get going. I'm sure this'll cost an arm and a leg. I'm already down to one eye, so I'd rather keep the other along with all my limbs, if you don't mind."

"All right, but there's an officer waiting outside. He said he needs to speak to you before you leave."

"Great. I can feel that headache coming back already," I muttered.

The doctor walked out of the room, closing the door behind him.

"Sorry, Mr. Trigger. I panicked. I—"

"That's enough of that, Zelda. You did what you had to do. I'm not cross with you. Don't worry."

A knock came at the door.

"Come in."

The door opened and a familiar face walked inside. He was what some people would call a mutt. A medium-sized dog of questionable parentage, mostly white with brown and black patches on his fur.

"Sergeant." I nodded.

He pointed to the rank on his uniform to silently correct me.

"Oh, Colonel now, huh? My mistake. I didn't know I was to be visited by a real big shot."

Me and Patches never really got along, but he was one of the precious few straight clean cops on the force. I heard he defended me when the whole incident at the department went down. I hadn't seen him since just before that.

"Trigger. Good to see you still have a knack for getting yourself into bad situations... and you still have that same smart mouth, too. You still don't know when to hold and when to fold. Sometimes it's a good idea not to run that mouth of yours, you know?"

"Thanks for the advice, mom. You come in here to bring me flowers and gab all day, or you got something you need to ask?"

"I overheard dispatch sending the rescue dogs over to your place. I thought I'd check in."

"They send a colonel to do that now?"

"Look, we had our differences, but you were a good cop. You should come by the station sometime. I've got a little more weight to throw around these days, so I might just be able to get your badge back."

I couldn't help but laugh. It looked like he has always had the same opinion of me as I did of him. Not a lot of love, but certainly plenty of respect.

"No thanks, Colonel. I appreciate you still thinking about me though. I really do. But why don't we just get that statement out of the way."

"Give it some thought."

He handed me a clipboard and a pen. I filled out all the information I had on Robby and Molly, and the stranger at the door. As well as I could remember, at least. I handed it back.

"This doesn't say anything about why you were there."

"Client confidentiality. My lips are sealed," I said, making the motion to zip up my mouth.

"All right, I can't make you give it up. What do you want to do about pressing charges?"

"Pick them up and have a good talk. They seemed like

decent enough kids, just scared to death of cops. We both know why."

He nodded. "All right. So no charges?"

"No charges."

"Take care of yourself, Trigger. Call us next time. We'll back you up."

"Give me your card, Colonel. I might call you, but just you and those you trust."

He handed me his card and left the room. The nurse came in a few minutes later, giving me my discharge papers complete with instructions on caring for my injuries. She said to take it easy for a couple of weeks. *Yeah, right.* I tossed those doctor's orders in the bin on my way out. I didn't have time to take it easy. I had work to do.

13

The next morning, I had Zelda ring up Lily, asking her to stop by the office. She showed up a short while later and Zelda buzzed her on in.

"Oh, detective, you look terrible! Are you all right?" Lily asked, seeming genuinely concerned.

"I'm all right now. Cost me a visit to the hospital. I think it warrants a renegotiation of the agreement, but we'll get to that in a minute. I got all this, believe it or not, courtesy of that maid of yours. Well, her boyfriend anyways," I explained.

"Oh, no! She didn't show up for work this morning. What happened?"

"Turns out she'd nabbed something from your stash—"

"My collar!"

I frowned and shook my head.

"No, ma'am. I'm afraid not." I reached into my desk, pulled out an envelope, and handed it to her. She opened it, pulling out the earrings and ring.

"Yes. Yes, these are mine. I hadn't noticed them missing. I just-"

"Yeah?"

"I just can't believe she stole them. It saddens me to think I may have to be more guarded."

"The kid don't have it easy. The harder somebody's got it, the harder it is not to resort to unsavory means to getting a full stomach. It shows you the true colors of a cat or dog. You see how they are when things are rough. If it's any consolation, she did seem to be remorseful. Whether it was because she got caught or because she realized it was the wrong thing to do, I couldn't say."

"Yes, that's true... but as far as payment goes, I'm afraid that I can't spare more than what I've already advanced you."

"You know, for such a good girl, Lily, you sure attract a lot of trouble. That two hundred you gave me will probably barely cover the hospital bill. Then I'm in the hole for my time after that. I'm afraid I'm out if we're not talking seven hundred for the deal, and another two hundred up front."

"You can't do that, detective. We had a deal and—"

"And what, Lily," I barked. "Riddle me this, Lily, if you would. Suppose you go to your favorite burger joint and order a burger. You pay at the register, right? Suppose you get home and discover the burger looks like it saw the oven this time last year. And the bread's moldy too. Do you say, 'Oh well, I guess we had a deal?'"

"Well, no, I—"

"Well, I got news for you, sister. That same principle applies here. I got my melon cracked good on account of this case. What's more is that I rent this building. So, I can't work for peanuts, but that's not even the issue here, since I don't need to explain my expenses to you. All I need to do is do the job you hired me for, and all *you* need to do is pay me for it."

"All right. I understand. Another one hundred up front and I'll owe you three hundred more when the job is done." She reluctantly reached into her purse and pulled out another one-hundred-dollar bill, handing it across.

"I said two hundred."

Lily stared at me in faux shock. She was hoping I'd be an easier mark than this it seems.

She dug into her purse and pulled out another bill. "Oh, yes. My apologies."

I took the bills and placed them in my pocket. "So, who else did you say had access to the room?"

"Just some members of my family. No one who would take anything that didn't belong to them."

This dame was way too trusting for her own good. "Do you remember what you said about the maid just the other day?"

"Yes. I suppose you're right, detective. Just my brother and my aunt." She hung her head and her voice got quieter.

"Either of them have cause for taking the collar?"

"No cause that comes to mind. No. Wait. Now that I think about it, my aunt Agatha wanted the collar when my mother passed!"

I tilted my head. "Why's that?"

"I think they shared the collar when they were children, so she thought it best that the collar goes to her."

"Bad enough to steal it?"

"Oh, goodness no. Oh... Well... Oh, I just don't know anymore! Perhaps? I don't even want to think about it." She cried and tried rubbing the tears away with her paws.

I took a tissue out of the box that sat on my desk, handing it to her. "I'll stop by to see her tomorrow."

"Should I let her know to expect you?"

"No, it would be best if you didn't. Just leave her address with Zelda on your way out. Let's hope your aunt doesn't give me a beating. Not sure I can take another one so soon."

To my surprise, she laughed. "Let's hope not. I'm not sure I could afford it."

14

The next morning I skimmed the paper to look for particular "mishaps." There was nothing out of the ordinary,
but plenty of mishaps. Oh, and there was Robby. "Assault
with a deadly weapon. Charges likely to be dropped."
Enough of that drivel.

I collected my coat and hat, setting out for the Rose
Garden Estates to see Agatha.

As I made my way closer, the reality hit me that I was
severely underdressed for this place. I'd heard of this
neck of the woods, but I never went to visit it in person. It
was one of those high-class neighborhoods you had to
pay to visit if you didn't live there. The was a hulking
hound at a booth who had to open a gate and let you
inside for five dollars. What a rip-off, but hopefully an
investment that paid off. Too bad Lily didn't mention that
up front. Was probably afraid I would ask for more of an
advance to cover it. I would have.

After taking a few turns down the winding streets I
finally arrived at my destination. What a place. Somehow,

I expected Lily's place probably wasn't too much different. Could've been in this same neighborhood, for all I
knew. Most likely. Funny how these rich types hold on to
a dime tighter than a mother holds onto a newborn pup.

This looked like a house you'd see on those checkout
line magazine covers. The ones for dames to get and then
show their husbands. It let him know what kind of home
she'd like to move into someday. Just a lot of big dreams. I
never was a fan of selling people on the big dreams like
that. Some people get a house like that, but the vast
majority of people in this city will never lay eyes on one
in person.

I knocked on the door.

A Doberman in a black dress answered. "Yes?"

"I'm here to see Agatha. She in?"

"Yes."

I stared at her for a moment, waiting for an invitation
inside. All she did was stare back. After a few seconds, I
gave up on the uncomfortable silence.

"Can I see her? I need to ask her some questions."

"Are you soliciting?"

"No, I'm a private detective."

This dame's stare was like getting a cold bucket of ice
water dumped on your head. It chilled you to the bone.

"You should know the Madam has very little patience
for uninvited guests, sir."

"Could you let her know Trigger is here to see her? I'll
keep it brief."

"One moment."

She stepped inside, and I waited at the door for a few
minutes. I sat on the steps and looked around to amuse

myself. Never saw the appeal in a place like this. Seemed like a great place for folks who thoroughly enjoyed being bored out of their minds. No pups or kittens playing in the yard, no bars or movie theaters nearby. Just other elderly dogs who also don't like visitors. When I get old, I want to keep doing what I was doing, just maybe a little slower and with more notes. If I managed to get old, that is.

"Mr. Trigger, please come in."

I walked in, and she took my coat and hat. After hanging them up, she motioned for me to follow her into the next room. It was like you'd imagine the living room of a wealthy old dog to look. Fancy paintings, rugs, glass tables. Nothing was out of place. Not a speck of dust to be seen anywhere. The silverware was probably real silver. Fine china was on display in dark wood cabinets. It was like no one actually lived here, this was just a model house for those magazine covers.

"Have you had your coffee this morning, sir?" The voice of an elderly dog coming from a chair on the other side of the room startled me. The back of the chair was facing me.

"I have, ma'am, thank you. I'd be happy to have another," I replied.

"Lady, please pour our guest a cup of coffee," the elderly dog said.

"Cream or sugar, sir?" Lady asked.

"Black. I like it black."

"As do I, sir. Now, I assume you are here to take care of my little problem?" Agatha asked.

I walked past the table, sitting in the chair across from

her. She was an old Chihuahua, who was white and looked strikingly similar to Lily. They were definitely family.

"Ma'am?"

"The ad in the paper which referred to the break-ins that have been happening around here recently."

A dog should never think or speak too quickly when faced with such an opportunity. On the one hand, this would give me an easy excuse to come back here. I could talk to the neighbors and tally a list of the things the thief had taken. If the collar was here, the thief might've encountered it. If they knew what they were doing, they swiped the collar too. If it's just some kid angry at the world and wanting to make trouble for the wealthy residents here, then it's just some easy money. And a dog could always use easy money.

On the other hand, if this was all unrelated, it would bog me down, making it so I couldn't get directly to the point or bring up the collar for a while. Unless...

"Yes, ma'am. I saw the ad this morning as a matter of fact. I've got a lot of experience with this sort of thing. Investigated several burglaries when I was on the force. Had an excellent track record too, if I may say so."

The Doberman stared at me with an uncomfortable amount of skepticism. Or maybe she didn't like me and it had nothing to do with skepticism. Or perhaps this is just how she looked at everyone all the time. She's lucky she had such a pretty face, otherwise that kind of staring could make a dog real uncomfortable. On second thought, maybe it makes it worse.

"Yes, I remember seeing an advertisement for your services some time ago. Why did you stop advertising?"

"Had to, as a measure to reduce the volume of clients, ma'am." I smiled my most convincing smile. I even showed a few teeth. Lady wasn't impressed.

"If you've such a volume of clients, then why did you make your way here?"

"I'll be frank with you, ma'am. Not all work is worth the same if you catch my meaning? I prefer to limit myself to cases where my caliber of services is required, and where the compensation aligns with that. We all got bills to pay, we all got to eat."

"Ha, isn't that the truth. I appreciate your candor, Mr..."

"Call me Trigger."

"Alright, Mr. Trigger. Let me get you up to speed on what happened. Then we'll talk about your fee."

15

"It started about a week ago at Ms. Autumn's house down the street. She was out for a walk on Sunday afternoon and came home to a dreadful mess. Many of her valuables were missing. You'll want to talk to her to get a complete list. The next day it was Mr. Rover's house. It was a mess again and the valuables were once again missing.

"Then, just two days ago, they burglarized my house while Lady and I were out shopping. They left a mess and valuables were missing. The neighbors and I are prepared to pool together a small fund for you, sir. Perhaps five hundred?"

These dogs probably blow five hundred on a fancy tea set. They really do keep their wallets sealed up so tight you couldn't blow it open with a stick of dynamite.

"I don't know, ma'am. As you can see, I'm already roughed up from handling a similar case. This occupation can get hazardous. A cornered thief will often use deadly force to escape. I'm sorry, ma'am, but about twice that amount would be more appropriate."

"Mr. Trigger, that seems excessive. All of our stolen valuables scarcely total that amount."

Yeah, right.

"I'm afraid that it would have to be at least seven-fifty, but good work requires fair pay."

She sighed, as though experiencing a significant defeat.

"I think I can convince the neighbors to increase their contributions. What do you require of an advance?"

"Three hundred, ma'am. I will also need a precise list from everyone so I can take an inventory of all the items missing. Your insurance will also ask for this, so you may already have one prepared."

"I'll prepare you a separate one. There are a few belongings I'd prefer to keep... private."

"Fair enough, ma'am, but do make sure I have the complete list. It's critically important that I have a complete inventory. The more confirmations I have of the thief's identity, the more likely we are to get an arrest and a conviction in court."

She paused, somewhat nervously, and looked at Lady.

"I understand."

She went into another room of the house and came back with a piece of paper. She handed it over and I scanned its contents eagerly. It wasn't an unusually long list; the sign of a somewhat slick burglar.

· · ·

One pair of diamond earrings, one carat diamond set in fourteen karat white gold

One silver teapot

Eight hundred dollars in cash

About twenty pieces of silver cutlery

One diamond ring, one and one half carat diamond set in fourteen karat white gold

One ruby-encrusted collar
      Three fourteen karat yellow gold necklaces

One electric radio

One golden turkey statue, one-of-a-kind

There it was, right before my very eyes. It was almost too easy. Except now, the problem was still finding the thing. Still, it's probably better it worked out this way since the dame wouldn't have let me have the collar even if I caught her red-handed. Lady, the muscle here, would've prevented me from getting it if I'd tried to swipe it myself.

"I bet that turkey statue fetches a high price, ma'am. And it's a unique piece?"

"Yes sir, you would be correct. It's by far the most expensive item on the list."

"It'll also be the easiest to identify. We catch someone carrying around a turkey statue, then we know we have our thief."

"So, when can you start?" Agatha asked.

"I intend to start right now."

"Splendid. Lady, show our detective to the door and pay him the advance."

"Thank you for the hospitality and the coffee, ma'am," I said as I reached out to shake her hand.

I followed Lady to the door where she collected my coat, hat, and my fee after disappearing briefly. This case was becoming a lot more of a tangled mess than I'd hoped for, but at least the money was turning out to be good. Can't complain about the good old two-for-one. Wasn't sure if it would thrill Lily or make her furious, but I wasn't eager to find out just yet. It's a shame the dame can't trust her aunt any more than she could trust her maid. Sometimes a dog's family ain't what it should be. You can choose your friends and your maid, but you can't choose your family.

16

After leaving Agatha's house, I made my way down the street to the first victim's home. This place was as high-class as any other house on the block. I walked up to the door and knocked. No answer. I waited for a moment before turning to walk away, then I heard the door open behind me.

"Can I help you?"

Wow, this lady was even older than Agatha. She looked like she was ready to kick the bucket at any moment, real frail looking. She was a Dachshund with a sagging back, a slow step, and a muzzle of snow white against her reddish coat. Not sure why she would even worry about getting her stuff back. Grandkids, maybe.

"Yes, ma'am. Agatha hired me to look into the burglaries recently," I said.

"Oh! Oh, please come in."

I followed her inside and hung my hat up on the hanger. What a mess. Unlike Agatha's house, her house was still littered with overturned furniture and items scattered all over the floor.

"Looks like you got hit pretty hard, ma'am."

"Oh yes, detective. It was just awful. I was out last Sunday afternoon and returned to find this terrible mess here in my very own home. What a shame you can't feel safe even in a neighborhood like this."

"Yes ma'am, I completely agree. Say, have any of you contacted the police yet?"

"Oh, yes. They say they'll be here in about a week." She grinned, but it was one of those grins someone gives you when they don't really want to grin. They want to ball up their fist and punch something. "You know, to fill out a report and refer me to the insurance company."

"Yes ma'am, I know how that show goes. Can you show me where the break-in happened?"

"Sure thing, detective. Right this way. What was your name?"

"Trigger, ma'am."

She took me around to the back of her house, and it was immediately obvious where the break-in happened. There was still a large open area where the glass was broken on her large sliding glass door. She had taken plastic and covered it. Poor dame. Did she not have anyone to help her clean this mess up?

"I see. That's some real nasty work on your door. Do you have a list made of what they took?"

"Yes. I've already made one for the insurance company. Please wait in the living room while I go fetch it for you. Oh, I apologize for being a poor host. Have you had your coffee yet today?" she asked.

"Yes, ma'am. I'm afraid if I had more it wouldn't be good for me. Thank you. You've been a perfectly fine host under the circumstances."

I walked back into the living room and sat on the couch. It wasn't long before she returned with the list. She handed it over and I scanned it with haste. Nothing particularly eye-catching, just a few pieces of assorted jewelry here and there. Since this was the perp's first haul out of the neighborhood, he must've been a little nervous and in a hurry. Only nabbed what he could grab fast and make it out quick with.

"And you never laid eyes on the perp. Is that right?"

"That's right. The fiend was in and out before I made it back home. I wish he'd taken some time to set the place back up before he left," she said, with that same I-want-to-punch-something grin. She might be feistier than I gave her credit for.

"All right, that should be about all I need. I'll be back in touch when I find something. Say, Ms. Autumn. Before I go, would you like some help putting this place back together?"

"Oh, I couldn't bother you with something like that. I'm sure someone will come by in the next few days to take care of it."

"Do you have any kids or grandkids coming by, Ms. Autumn?"

"No, all of them have moved out of Black District. Thankfully."

"So it's just you here?"

"You make it sound something awful. I quite like it

though. I have this nice place in this nice neighborhood where I can just relax."

"You put it that way, and it actually sounds pretty nice. All right, I'm not due to meet Mr. Rover for at least another couple of hours. I may as well help you straighten this place up. Better than just walking around with my hands in my pockets waiting."

I had no appointments. I just didn't want to admit that I was putting off my paycheck to help an old lady clean her house. That kind of thing might damage my reputation as a tough-as-nails private detective. Couldn't let that get out.

17

I knocked on the door. A dog not much older than me answered. I assumed it was one of his employees.

"Is Mr. Rover in?"

"You're looking at him."

"You're Mr. Rover?"

"Did I stutter?"

"You look a little younger than what I was expecting. Don't expect to see a young pup like yourself already in a big fancy neighborhood like this. Anyway, I've been hired to investigate the burglaries that have taken place here recently. I've already been to Agatha's house and Autumn's. I wondered if I might come in and ask you a few questions."

"No, you may not. This is my only day off. I'd rather not spend it gabbing with some rent-a-cop. Not everyone in this neighborhood is retired, you know. Some of us still owe the bank money for the roof over our head."

I shook off the cop comment with ease. Real original. Not like it was the first time I'd heard that one.

"Sure, I understand. Could you at least give me a list of what they stole from your place? Or do you want to play hardball about that too?"

His eyes lit up a little. "There's some fire in you after all. Sure. Let me go get it."

He went back inside the house, then came out a few moments later with a piece of paper. He handed it to me, wished me luck, and slammed the door in my face. A real piece of work, this guy. I looked the list over. I was correct that the perp improved with his second hit. He got some cash from Mr. Rover, and a small safe he found in one of his closets. Looked like he also got some of the wife's jewelry. Nothing particularly noteworthy though. Seemed the turkey statue and the collar would be my best lead.

I made my way back to the office. I greeted Zelda when I came into the door. I asked her to ring up Lily to come by for an update. While I waited, I went back into my office to make notes and review the evidence of the burglary case. The intercom buzzed on my desk a couple of hours later.

"Trigger, Lily's here to see you."

"Send her in."

She walked in and sat down.

"I've heard you've been busy, detective."

"You heard, huh? I was in your neck of the woods today."

"I also found out that my aunt has hired you to look into the burglaries there."

"She has. You kept your mouth shut about me working for you when she mentioned it, I'd hope."

"Yes. I'm not quite that foolish. I trust you enough that I assumed you had your reasons."

I nodded.

"Well..." She stared at me blankly.

"Yes?"

"What are your reasons?"

"Just that. My reasons."

"Not if I'm paying you," she snapped back.

"Promise you can keep your head about you if I explain?"

"I'm not one to lose my temper."

"All right." I slid the missing item list across the table to her. "Have a look."

She held it up in front of her and glanced over it before putting it back down on the table. She sighed and closed her eyes, rubbing her forehead with her paw.

"Good thinking. Except now we're back to square one."

"We're back to square one, that's true. But at least this extra work won't cost you any extra money. Your aunt will pay me to take it from here."

"I'm now afraid that I may never see it again."

"I won't lie to you. That's a real possibility. The collar may have already changed hands three times by now. It may already be out of Black District. It could still be in the thief's possession and they're too nervous to sell easily identifiable items. Just no way to know how it'll play out. I'll tell you, though, that I do still have hope in finding it."

"Good, that makes me feel better. If you think there's

a chance I'll accept that. Thank you, detective. Anything else?"

"Not at the moment. I'll keep you updated. Do your best to make sure your aunt doesn't find out I'm working for you."

"I should be able to manage that. So long."

"Leave your address with Zelda on the way out in case I need to stop by. Keep your doors and windows locked, and be careful."

"You should consider staking out the neighborhood."

"I don't like to give up the sleep. Makes me cranky."

She gave me a scowl.

"Detective…"

I held up my hands as if to stop the force of her look from knocking me out of my chair.

"All right. All right. I'm just fooling. It's not a bad idea. Maybe I'll do just that."

18

I had Zelda ring up Agatha. I needed a security pass so I could come and go as I pleased without having to pay that hound five bucks each time. Within a few hours, we got a ring back from the dog who was out front when I last visited. He let me know they'd agreed to issue me a resident's pass that I could pick up whenever I wanted. I'd have to frame that thing in my office when all of this was over, telling folks that's where I lived. Talk about the big times.

I headed on over there and the security dog met me at the gate.

"Mr. Trigger, welcome back. I was about to make the rounds to inform the residents of your plans to stake the place out."

"Now why would you do a thing like that?"

"We don't want it to alarm the residents if they see you out."

"And if one of the residents is the burglar?"

He paused for a moment, looking down in deep thought.

"Well, yes, Mr. Trigger. I hadn't thought about that. Yes, you're right." *And that's why I get paid the big bucks.*

He handed me the resident's pass; I put it into my pocket.

"I'll be around then, but probably not until tomorrow night," I said. "Do me a favor and don't send out a memo about it."

It would be tonight. Only I didn't really trust any dog or cat all that much in this whole situation. What if the perp knew the security dog, and that dog tipped him off? Not a risk I was willing to take just now.

I walked on up to Agatha's place to make sure she didn't rat the plan out to anybody else. According to her, she had told no one apart from the security guard. I made sure she knew to keep it that way. Once that was sorted, I scouted out the proper hiding spot. I then went home to my apartment to sneak in a quick nap, coming back when it was good and dark.

It was one of those misty moonlit nights that felt cold even though it was summer. It was the kind of night that makes a dog want to howl at the moon, only he can't because he'll blow his cover. It was also one of those instincts one was expected to suppress in modern, polite society. I had a full view of the whole place, from the hill on the edge of the neighborhood. I got behind a bush to make sure no one could see me from below. If anything happened, I would see it from here.

I sat there quietly for several hours. You could hear a

pin drop on a night like this, even on dirt. It seemed like this would be a reasonably peaceful, uneventful night. That was until I felt something pointy jamming into the small of my back, and a dame's voice coming from behind me. She was disguising it. A cat? Must've been to sneak up on me like that.

"Beautiful night, isn't it, detective?"

I wasn't sure what she had jammed into my back, so I didn't turn around to see who it was. Things were piecing themselves together a little better now. What I was dealing with here was a real professional. Made everything look like real sloppy work, even though she could've left the place spotless. Smart. Fooled me good.

"So, who was it that tipped you off that I'd be here? Was it the security dog?" I asked.

"You're a little duller than I was expecting."

"Was it Agatha? Come on, don't keep me here in suspense all night."

"Oh, I wouldn't do that. What's the hurry? Got somewhere else you need to be?"

"Yeah, since I won't be sneaking up on you, at home, asleep in my bed."

"Well, it's a little late for that, isn't it? Look, detective, I really don't want to kill you. So, why don't you walk away and pretend you never heard anything? I'll come back another night, no harm no foul."

"You know I can't do that," I said.

"I thought you might say as much. Good night."

She put a precise paw chop to the side of my neck. An expert move. I hit the ground like a sack of potatoes and was out like a light. By the time I came to, it was breaking daylight. At least the dame had the courtesy not to whack me in the head. My guess is this cat must've been after that statue, and everything else was an elaborate cover up with a lot of collateral damage. What a night...

19

After I collected my bearings and my hat, I headed down the hill to speak to the on-duty security guard. He was a Jack Russell Terrier, bright in the eyes and big in the mouth.

"Who are you?"

"Trigger, private detective."

"Right, thought you wouldn't be here until tonight."

"I changed my mind. Didn't want anybody tipping off the perp," I said.

"Well, you don't have to worry about me, detective. Not at all. I'm on the straight and narrow. Live strictly inside the law."

"If you were a criminal would you tell me?" I smirked. "To tell you the truth, I didn't think anyone tipped her—"

"You mean the robber's a dame!?"

"That's right. I could tell by—"

"Get a glimpse of her? She good looking? Single?" He winked.

"You into cats, Mr...?"

"Danny, detective. Name's Danny, and no sir."

"Cut the wisecracks then, will you? I need to use your phone."

I pulled out Patches' number from my pocket and dialed his direct line.

"ACPD. How may I direct your call?"

"Need to speak to Colonel Patches. Isn't this his direct line?"

"Colonel Patches is out looking into a case. This is dispatch. Shall I take a message or transfer you to an available officer?"

"No. No message. I'll call back."

I hung up the phone.

"Hey, Danny, anyone report a break in last night?"

"Not yet, and I didn't hear any commotion," he replied.

Just then I spotted a few dogs in uniform coming down the road toward the gate. I recognized one of them. So this was the case Patches was working.

"Nice of you to show up, Colonel."

"Trigger." He nodded. "I heard the residents here had hired a private detective to take care of the burglary problem, so I thought I'd come by and see for myself."

"Looks like it's more the other way around. Believe it or not, I just tried to call you."

"Oh, you did, did you? Finally growing out of some of that stubbornness?"

"I guess you can say that."

"Let me introduce you to the officers I've assigned to this case. This is Lieutenant Petey and Lieutenant Buddy."

"All right. Here's what I know. Last Sunday was a break in down the street here. Lady named Autumn's house. It was while she was out Sunday afternoon running errands. Looked like a real amateur job. Real sloppy, but that was just a ruse. No, now don't look at me like that. It'll make sense in a minute. So, the second one was the next day at this other dog's, Rover's, house. Also made to look real amateur. Now, here's the kicker. The third day our burglar visits Agatha's house, the one who hired me. When she gave me her insurance list for the items that were missing, there were a couple of unique items on the list. One, in particular, was this statue. A golden turkey.

"Now, I was thinking at first that this must've been a small statue. Either way, it's made of gold, right? Well, you see, now I'm thinking maybe it's a little bigger than that. See, I met our burglar last night when I was staking the place out. The broad snuck up right behind me when I hid in some bushes on the hill up there. It was quiet last night. I'm a real cautious dog to boot, and I've got good ears. Stuck something in my back and told me not to turn around. She gabbed at me for a couple of minutes, put a clean shot with her paw to my neck and knocked me full out. She also had the sense to not go through with what she was planning last night. This fit the profile of any current suspects?"

Patches looked puzzled. "To tell you the truth, we suspected Rico when we first heard they hit this neighborhood. Then we heard they made a mess, so we thought it was just some punk kid fooling around. Now you're telling us it is a professional after all, but it's not Rico. That really throws a spin on it."

"So, I take it you boys don't have any leads on a lady cat burglar around these parts?" I asked.

Patches shook his head. "The problem isn't that we don't have one. The problem is that we have too many."

I scratched my head when a thought crossed my mind. "Say, Colonel, what if this dame didn't abandon her target last night? What if she wasn't here to rob a place? What if she was here to meet someone and just happened to notice me?"

Lieutenant Buddy nodded. "You know, I was actually just thinking the same thing. Otherwise, how would this dame know about that statue you were talking about in the first place?"

I pointed at him, a grin on my face. "Exactly! All right boys, if you'll be so kind as to humor me, here's what I think we should do. You boys just stick to the routine for now. Interview, document, report, etc. I'll do a little more digging into the value of this statue, and where it might've come from. That'll give us a better idea of who we're dealing with. Oh, and let me give you my card. Call me if you hear anything, and I'll do the same."

I headed back to the office for the day without telling anyone else what happened. Best if I let them do their job without getting in the way. Besides, I had plenty on my plate already.

20

I went back to my apartment to snag a quick nap before heading back to the office. As usual, Zelda greeted me with cheer when I walked inside, but this time she had a letter in her paw.

"Someone left this in our mailbox this morning. It has your name on it. No return address. I thought it was strange, so I didn't open it."

Was this what I thought it was? "Thanks. You were right not to open it. At least, if it's what I think it is." I took it to my office and put on a pair of gloves. I opened it as carefully as I could, slid the letter out of the envelope, and read the handwritten note aloud.

Trigger,

You're a smart dog, so no doubt you already knew who this letter was from the moment you saw it. I noticed you had a head injury when we last met, so consider that my one good deed. You're welcome.

I wanted to do you the courtesy of informing you that I won't be hitting anything else in that neighborhood since I already got what I came for. But I'm sure you've figured that part out.

Stop by and see me in the Adria District. Let's make a game of it, detective. See if you can catch me.

Bad Kitty

Bad Kitty, eh? Bad Kitty suits her; though, I think she gave me a little more credit than I deserved. Based on what I knew, I wasn't even close to having enough to find her. Or did I? She seemed to think I might. Maybe I missed something, or maybe she's just making wisecracks. At any rate, now the collar was probably long gone. I wasn't surprised that the statue would wind up somewhere in Adria District, but what about all the common jewelry, the radio - things like that? They'd laugh at all that in Adria. Maybe even toss it in a dumpster. No, she probably got rid of the small stuff quick here before leaving. Low risk and no chance of identifying it. The collar was different, though. It wasn't as expensive as the statue. Not by a long shot. Maybe just enough to make it into Adria.

I rang up Lieutenant Buddy and had him come by to

pick up the letter to lift any prints and check it for any hidden clues. I remembered one case where the type of paper used ended up busting the guy. You never know with this kind of stuff. I didn't have my hopes up.

After that, I rang Lily up to give her the bad news about the collar. I could hear the heartbreak in her voice, but she took it pretty well. I told her I had business that might soon come up in Adria, so I'd keep my eye out for it there. She didn't exactly sound hopeful. She thanked me for all the work I'd put into finding it. It's a shame I wouldn't have an excuse to see her again soon. I was getting used to seeing her face here in the office from time to time. It was a face that was pretty easy to get used to.

I went back down to Rose Garden and talked to Agatha. I only got another hundred bucks out of her for the job, on account of not being able to recover any of the stolen items. Was a real shame, although I did find out more about that turkey statue. She called it the Grand Gobbler. Should've named it the Twenty-Grand Gobbler, cause that's about what it was worth according to her. She said she'd kept it a secret on account of it standing out, even in a luxurious place like this. She joked that it was hard to afford the insurance premium on it, but she was glad she paid it. I bet.

I left my card for her to pass on to the insurance investigator who would come by. I figured they would send a real mean one, one of those stiff, bookish types. You don't pay out a policy like that without trying to discover any foul play.

I really enjoyed the peace and quiet that filled the next few weeks. I did a lot of sitting back with my feet on my desk, listening to the radio; gave my skull a chance to heal too. I got that Rose Garden Estates residential pass framed like I planned. Stuck it right up on the wall in my office. Made an excellent joke for everybody that came in.

Nothing ever came back on Bad Kitty's letter. They kept it on file in case they compared handwriting down the road. Bad Kitty wasn't the only master thief I'd met in my career, or recently, who liked to play these games. But her game would have to wait. I would once again be tangled up with another master thief by the name of Rico.

I picked up the paper and didn't even have to open it up. I knew immediately I was looking at the one I'd been waiting for, right there on the front-page headline. The largest movie theater in Adria had been temporarily closed to investigate a major incident. The article said a whole lot of nothing about what happened with the incident, which, as I've learned, means that what happened was probably very inconvenient for Mr. B. I took the story as my cue to hit the road.

Sure enough, I received a visitor the next day.

"Mr. Trigger, there's a gentleman here to see you," Zelda said.

"Send him in."

A well-fed-looking pooch walked into my office. I feared for the safety of my chair but asked him to take a seat anyway. He was a bulldog, broad as he was tall, but had a look of health and strength about him. Perhaps it was the expensive three-piece suit he was wearing; still, he managed to look both nervous and confident at the same time. He had his head held high with his chest out but also clenched his teeth fiercely. Where had I seen him before?

"What can I do for you?" I asked.

"You read the papers, detective?"

"I do."

"Then you have no doubt read about what transpired in my theater in Adria."

"*Your* theater?"

"Yes, the Starlight Theater. I'm the owner."

I knew a big shot like this had to be playing ball with Mr. B. Like everyone else in this city, he's in it for himself.

"So you're looking to hire a private detective to look into it?"

"That's right."

"Someone recommend me to you?"

"Not in particular. Your name just kept coming up,

and you see, this is a very sensitive matter of which I would rather not involve the police."

"I think I know what you mean, Mr..."

"Brutus. Name's Brutus. Sorry for not introducing myself when I came in, but you understand I have a lot on my mind."

"Yes, I would imagine you do. How can I fit into all this?"

"As I said, I would like to hire you. I'd be willing to pay you double your usual rate," Brutus offered.

"Well, there really is no usual rate, Brutus. That all depends on the nature of the case - how convoluted, and how hazardous for my health the case happens to be. So how about you start by telling me what actually happened?"

"All right, but I need your word this conversation will remain confidential. I don't want any of this getting to the police or the independent press."

"We always keep things confidential here. You don't need to worry about that," I said.

"I'll start with the main event and tell you what I know from there. As we discussed, what you saw in the paper is only a half-truth at best. See, we had planned to play a movie we had produced ourselves. It painted Mr. B in a very positive light. We hoped it would keep things running smoothly, keep business good for everybody. It's not that Mr. B is my favorite kind of character, detective, rather it's that you can't be on his bad side if you want to do business in Adria. However, a different movie played when we ran the reels on Thursday. Now keep in mind that, while all this was going on, we had filled the seats with some of Mr. B's top cats and dogs. All watching with bated breath."

He wiped the sweat from his brow with a handkerchief from his jacket pocket.

"You all right, Mr. Brutus?"

He nodded, taking a deep breath before continuing.

"What emerged from the speakers was a voice that identified Mr. B as a scourge to both the district and the city. It didn't pull any punches. I tried to signal to the employee standing at the reel to shut it off, but he couldn't hear in that room. I ended up having to run upstairs myself and turn it off, but by then everyone was good and riled. We hadn't disclosed what our film would be about or what the message would be. Of course, they thought we were trying to make some kind of stand, some kind of big statement. Only we weren't!"

"I get it. You're innocent and someone framed you. What else?"

"Now I'm in serious hot water. I told one of Mr. B's cats I would stake my business and reputation on this being a setup. He said he would give me the opportunity to prove it, but they closed my theater until I could do just that. Nobody's happy when the theater is closed, detective. Least of all, me. Folks might go to a new theater, and I'm losing buckets of money every day we're not open."

"Then I suppose you wouldn't mind sharing a bucket or two with me then?"

"Now that you've heard what I've had to say, how does two thousand dollars sound? One thousand up front."

"Been a while since I've been to Adria, Brutus, but

from what I remember, a thousand dollars won't take a dog very far."

He was sweating even more now. You could almost see the gears turning in his mind. Trying to get money out of these rich types really was like trying to pull teeth from a turnip.

He scowled. "I suppose you can't be expected to travel all around Adria on your own dime. Here's what I'll do for you. My company has a charge account at nearly every major establishment in the district. I'll give you one of those cards. All your expenses. Entertainment, food, drinks, a place to stay - whatever you can think of. I'll cover it and write it off as a company expense. Though, I hope you won't get too carried away. This way you keep every dime you make and have yourself a good time along the way I hope. Sound fair?"

This dog was desperate. In reality, he probably just multiplied his offer by five or ten. Day-to-day expenses in Adria were huge. Talk about going outside of your comfort zone...

"That'll be sufficient, Mr. Brutus. You just hired yourself a detective."

He all but jumped to his feet and extended his paw. "When can you start?"

I took it with a firm grasp. "Tomorrow."

Odds were good that some of Agatha's stolen items, along with their thief, made their way to Adria too. It might also include one ruby collar. This was my chance to find out, and maybe change my luck in the process.

22

After Mr. Brutus gave me my advance and left, I advanced Zelda a month of pay too. She was happy, until I let her know we'd be shutting down for a time. I wanted to make sure I paid her all the way through, and I could afford to with the advance I got. After that, I went about finding a suit in my closet. Just one suit. Brutus could pay for the other two when I got there.

It was a long walk to Adria. Took most of the day to get there. Talk about a sight to behold. High walls surrounded the district. It looked a lot more like a fortress than a city district. Cats were loitering outside the gate, probably hoping to pickpocket one of the work passes into the district. Brutus told me to guard mine like a first-born pup. At the gate, a sharply dressed pooch asked to see my pass. He slid it through some kind of machine and the gate opened automatically. Two Rottweilers holding some type of long weapon I'd never seen before stood on either side of the gate. The things looked like metal poles with two prongs coming off the end. Probably those new shock sticks I've been hearing about. I wasn't keen to find out, though.

You could hear music playing the moment you walked in; it was coming out of the various establishments that lined the streets near the gate. Everybody looked loaded. Seemed to be having a great time while stumbling out of these places. It became a calmer, more serious place as I got farther away from the gate. The party joints gave way to clothing stores, radio shops, jewelry stores, and more. After stopping several times to ask for directions, I finally made my way to the Starlight Theater to see Brutus.

This place really looked like it belonged. It was at least ten times bigger than the biggest movie theater we had back home. A big Rottweiler greeted me at the door and told me that Brutus was expecting me. When I stepped inside, an expansive purple carpet greeted me. There wasn't a stain to be seen. All the furniture looked to be made of oak with a beautiful lacquer finish with every print painstakingly wiped away. Along the top of all the counters was gold trimming, which I suspected wasn't imitation. Once we made it into Brutus's office, he appeared to be in much better spirits than he was the last time I saw him.

"Mr. Trigger, so very glad you made it. What's your impression of the district so far?"

"It's quite an upscale place, Mr. Brutus. However, probably best I not elaborate on my overall impression."

He laughed. "I think I know exactly what you mean, detective. So, are you ready to get started?"

"Let's start by interviewing your boy who was in

charge of changing the reel. Do you have a private office I can use while I'm investigating? I prefer these interviews to be one-on-one."

"I'm a little hesitant to let you do that, but if that's what it takes for you to do your best work, then I'll have a private office prepared for you." He looked to the big dog that had escorted me inside and said, "Show Mr. Trigger to the office down the hall."

I started to figure out what was going on with the big dog when he escorted me to an office that was only a few doors down. One I might've easily shown myself to. I suppose it's understandable. I'm not sure I'd fully trust me either, given the circumstances.

"Hey big guy, got a name?"

"The name's Marty, detective, but keep in mind Mr. Brutus isn't paying me for small talk. You probably figured out by now I'm being paid to keep an eye on you. So, don't try anything funny while you're here."

"Wouldn't dream of it, Marty. Also, you never know. You and I might be good friends by the time this is over."

He laughed out loud, breaking the stoic demeanor he had been carrying. "The moon just might come crashing down and smash right into this theater, Mr. Trigger. You just never know about these kinds of things. Let me go fetch the gentleman."

I looked around the office trying to imagine what this manager's life might have been like. Did he have a family? Evidently, he had a nice place to live. I wonder what the residential area in a place like this might look like. Side-by-side mansions spanning for miles into the horizon? No, probably nothing so extreme. I bet they looked a little better than my apartment though. A lot of the people who worked in Adria didn't live in the district. They come here and worked their day, then leave the district and go home if they live close enough. Still, even some dogs who were big shots outside the district were fighting tooth and nail for a chance to come to a place like this and sweep the floors. That's why the closer you got to Adria's gates, the nicer the homes were in the Black District.

I once knew an accountant in my neck of the woods who tried for six months only to finally get a job waiting tables at a restaurant here. Worked there for a year, chatting people up on his lunch break, meeting people. Then he landed the biggest client of his career. Said he paid more than the next thirty clients below him combined. After that, he had all but retired. He worked with the one guy from Adria when he needed him. That's one of those rare feel-good stories though. Most of the time, kids came here with big eyes and big hearts, getting promptly used up by the city and thrown away when they're done. Most of those who live here will only do business with the people they grew up with. So there's not much room for the outsider to come in. Guess you could say that with almost everybody. I'd like to think I gave everyone a fair shake.

23

"All right, Trigger, here's your dog. His name's Tuffy. He's the one Mr. Brutus told you about."

Tuffy was a Pomeranian who was allergic to eye contact and sitting still. That didn't mean much in this kind of situation, though. I was a little nervous myself. Besides, Tuffy had that distinct "fall guy" look. Young pup and tense; he was in the right place at the right time.

"Have a seat, Tuffy. I'd like to ask you a few questions." I pointed to the chair across from me. Marty gave him an impolite shove, and he went over to have a seat.

"You gotta believe me, mister. I didn't do it. I didn't have nothing to do with that reel. Either of 'em, swear it."

"My name's Trigger, private detective. I only want to ask you a few questions. Take it easy."

He took a deep breath and put on his best fake calm face.

"Sometimes going in order is a little boring, Tuffy, so let's take these questions as they pop into my head. Let's start with why you didn't change the reel when Mr. Brutus was trying to get your attention to change it."

"It's like I told Mr. Brutus. I can't hear real well up in that room."

I signaled for Marty to leave, but he wouldn't budge.

"Did you forget that your boss said I could have these one-on-one interviews?"

He looked like he wanted to bite my head off. "You're right, Mr. Trigger. Where are my manners?" He stepped out of the office and closed the door.

"Now, where were we? Oh, you were just telling me that big fat lie about not being able to hear Brutus up in the booth."

"Mr. Trigger, you gotta believe me. I–"

"I gotta believe nothing, kid. Least of all the big fat lies being told right to my face. Care to try again?"

"All right, detective, you win. It's true you can't hear well up in the booth, but you can hear a little. Maybe I liked what I heard, all right? Maybe I agreed with it."

"So, you act like you can't hear any of it. You made sure not to look toward Brutus so you wouldn't see him signaling for you to turn it off. That about right?"

He crossed his arms. "Yeah. That's about right."

"So how do you figure into bringing the new reel in here?"

"I don't figure into it. So maybe I liked their work. I didn't have anything to do with bringing it in here."

I leaned over and pointed my paw in his face. "Who else besides you handles the reels?"

"What's your angle in all this, Detective?" he squealed.

"I'm angling to get paid, kid."

He threw his paws in the air. "That's the problem. This whole situation with Mr. B. I got no problem with making money. It's why I'm here too. The problem is when it's all you care about. Problem is when you're willing to do anything for a dime."

I didn't disagree with the kid, but I couldn't say so. "That's a nice speech there, Tuffy. Only you still didn't answer my question. Who else handles the reels?"

He lowered his head, defeated. "All right. It's easy to see you got a wad of cash where your heart should be, just like everyone else in this city. We've got a maintenance dog who moves the boxes where they need to go after they get shipped in. Then there's the guy who ships 'em in, beyond that the distribution company, beyond that the production company. Need me to go on?"

"They pay you extra for your wisecracks, Tuffy?"

"No, sir. We done?"

"Yeah, for now."

Tuffy stood up and walked out of the room in a huff. I called Marty back into the office.

"Get anything good out of the guy?" Marty asked.

"Wouldn't be able to tell you if I did."

"That how you're going to play it, detective?"

"That's how I'm playing it."

He looked as though his head would pop at any moment. A thinly disguised growl lay on his lips, but he had about as much of a chance of keeping that act up as a boulder floating in a pond.

"Is the maintenance guy in?"

"Probably."

"Be a sport and fetch him for me. I need to ask him a few questions."

24

It took Marty all of ten minutes to get back to the room with suspect in tow. The suspect was a Chihuahua like me. Almost solid brown with a patch of white fur around his left eye. I motioned for him to sit down.

"You must be the dog that does the maintenance around here. What's your name?" I asked.

He sat down across from me like he had done a thousand times before. "Name's Brownie. Can we make this quick? I gotta get back to work."

"That's up to you, Brownie. This could take all day if we feel like it - right, Marty?"

Marty rubbed the knuckles on his paw enthusiastically. "Yeah, I got nowhere else to be."

Brownie looked back and forth between Marty and I, letting loose a big laugh. "Don't you think you're starting the tough-cop routine a little early?"

"Since neither of us are cops, I don't know how well that'll go over," I replied.

"Well, out with it. Make hay while the sun still shines and all that."

"You seem awfully experienced with these kinds of interviews," I stated.

"So you called me in here for an interview... to ask me why I seem experienced with doing interviews?"

"No, this is just a bonus question. Satisfying my curiosity."

"So, you're not a cop?"

"You remember how I said earlier that this could either go quick or we could take all day?"

"Yeah."

"If you keep answering every question with another question, I'll have to ask Marty to get us a couple of pillows and a bunk bed."

He smirked, turning his face. "Fire away, detective."

"You're familiar with the swapping incident, correct?"

"I think that's pretty obvious. Want to just skip to the real question?"

"No, I know exactly what I asked. I want to know how familiar you are with the switching incident."

"I orchestrated the whole thing. I had the fake reel made. Got it smuggled in here too. Would you believe me if I told you that?"

"I might. I get paid either way. All I have to do is pin it on somebody and that sounded like a confession to me. A pretty good one to boot. That sound like a good enough confession to you, Marty?"

"More than good enough for me." Marty grinned.

"Well, there you have it. Let's give the cops a ring and

we'll wrap this all up. Whole case solved before supper time. How about that?"

Brownie's charismatic smile faded into a quivering frown, just like the schoolyard bully beaten in front of his friends by the runt. It looked like I had succeeded in making him nervous. Nervous dogs always make mistakes.

"Okay, now hold on! I'll tell you that I'm not your man, just in case you really are interested in solving this. I didn't have anything to do with the reel swapping."

"Oh? You're awfully forthcoming with the information now, Brownie."

"I had my fun, detective, but now I'm telling you the truth. All I do is unbox the things when they come in. I take them to the right room or take the whole box to the right room if it all goes to the same place. I don't check them. I box the old ones up and I unbox the new ones. I put the new ones on the machine if I'm asked to; if I'm not asked to, then I don't even open the box."

"Were you asked to when the switch happened?"

Brownie looked down for a moment, trying to remember. "You know what? I wasn't. I wasn't asked to open them that night."

"All right, Brownie. You're free to go for now."

He stood up, nodded, and hustled out of the room. Something about him didn't feel right. He was definitely hiding something. I went back to Mr. Brutus's office and got his address. Something told me it would be worth following him home to get a closer look. You learn from experience doing this job that it's best not to ignore your instinct. It rarely steers you wrong.

25

I kept my distance as I followed him through the various corridors of Adria. We eventually wound up at what appeared to be a small, abandoned storage building nestled in the middle of several larger buildings. That made it conveniently difficult to spot from a distance. After he approached the door, he entered a code onto a keypad. I was too far away to see what he'd entered, but this whole case was getting more interesting by the minute. When he pressed the last button there was a loud click, and the door snapped slightly ajar. After Brownie entered and closed the door behind him, I made my way around the building to see if I could find a way inside, or at least a way to see what was going on in there. The best I saw was a ventilation fan about midways up on the building on the back side. Not ideal, but it would have to suffice.

As quietly as I could, I moved whatever boxes and crates I could find nearby into something resembling a pyramid I could climb onto. I climbed atop my shaky tower and peered inside. Too bad the fan was running. It covered up any noise I made, sure, but I couldn't hear a doggone thing. There were several tables in the room with machines on top with a couple of dogs and cats on each side tinkering away. I had to watch for a while before I realized what was going on. At first, it looked like they were repairing slot machines, but it became clear after I saw one move over to a testing table. They pulled the lever bizarrely, almost like a code, and it would come up jackpot every time. They were rigging the machines.

I climbed down quietly as I could and made my way to the nearest payphone. I phoned Lieutenant Buddy and told him what was going on. He was quiet for a moment before he told me he'd better let me talk to Patches.

"You say you're where, Trigger?"

"Adria, Colonel. I've got a whole warehouse full of slot-machine fixers ready for your boys to come and haul off."

"I'll give you a fair warning about Adria. The chief doesn't let the rest of us go there. He allows only Colonel Bones and his men to police there. My hands are tied."

"All right, so do I even need to guess what kind of dog Bones is?"

"Do you?"

I sighed. "How big of a problem is this guy?"

"Look, why don't you meet him for yourself? You'll see what I mean. Just call back and ask to speak to Colonel Bones. But Trigger, remember one thing: he's not on your side."

"Thanks for the warning." I hung up.

I dialed back a minute later and asked to be transferred to Colonel Bones. A very cheery voice greeted me on the other line. He said to hang tight and wait. It didn't take long for them to arrive in full force. About twenty dogs burst through the door and arrested everyone inside. As they were still marching everyone out, I finally got my chance to meet Colonel Bones.

"You must be the one who tipped us off. What brought you here?"

"Name's Trigger, Colonel. Brutus, the owner of the Starlight, hired me to look into the incident that happened at his theater recently."

"And how's that going?"

"Too early to say, but I think it's going pretty well. Earlier today I interviewed the guy who works maintenance at the theater. I thought he acted strange, so I followed him here. I was hoping to find something to do with the reels, but instead I found this. I'm sure a fella such as yourself can appreciate the opportunity to bring a bunch of criminals to justice."

"We do appreciate the tipoff, Trigger." For a moment there, I thought maybe Patches had him all wrong; or maybe he exaggerated. That feeling, however, didn't last long. "For one, these guys weren't paying their fair share to Mr. B to conduct this kind of business in Adria. Second, Mr. B has a big casino down the street. If these rigged machines were going where I think they were that would be terrible for Mr. B's business. Wouldn't you agree?"

It amazed me how open he was with his allegiance to Mr. B. I knew things were bad in Adria, but he said all that without a single hint of concern in his voice. Bones must have felt invincible. Maybe he was, or maybe this kind of overconfidence was the gap in his armor.

"I suppose it would be."

He put his paw on my shoulder, lowering his voice. "You understand what I'm driving at?"

And there it was. The veiled threat I'd been expecting. "Colonel, you make yourself crystal clear."

What a mess this whole thing was turning out to be. My case was showing all the usual signs of one about to go cold. I was working blind in the first place; I'd still gotten no direction from Rico, and now I couldn't count on any help from the cops. But that was a familiar predicament for me. I took the night off and enjoyed myself a little on Brutus's dime. My first day here had turned out to be a productive one.

There was a unique joint just down the street from the theater I'd passed on my way in called Sweet Dreams. So I headed down to have a look. It was a lively place with a steady flow of young dogs and cats coming and going. Definitely not a place I'd normally find myself. Give me a newspaper and a cup of joe over a loud party any day of the week. I got more than plenty of excitement from work. At the end of the day, all I wanted to do was kick my feet up and enjoy some peace and quiet.

I walked up to the entrance and tried to get in the honest way. The guy at the door told me to get lost. I waited a few minutes for the shift change, went back to the door and told the guy I was one of Brutus's cousins. I flashed my card, and with enthusiasm, he showed me right inside.

It was a sight to behold. Seeing was about all you could do. There was a band playing and people talking loudly everywhere. Yelling, to be more precise. I sat down at the bar and ordered myself a warm milk and a cut of salmon. That seemed to be this joint's unique appeal. Milk, strawberries, and fish. It said on the menu this was the only place you could buy them. Throw in music and dancing; you get yourself prime real estate for dogs and cats to spend their parents' hard-earned money. As I was waiting for my meal, a painting hanging above the bar caught my eye. It was a beagle in a snazzy suit, one arm tucked behind his back, the other holding out a glass of milk. Why did he look so familiar?

As the bartender made his way back over, I motioned toward it. "Say, who's the pooch in the painting?"

He chuckled. "You mean you don't know?"

"Would I have asked if I did?"

"No, don't suppose you would. That's the boss, Rick. Owns this joint, and a whole lot more. You could count the number of dogs with more money that him on one paw. Now, if we're done shouting trivia you can eat your meal and I can get back to work."

The bartender slid the plate and the glass over. I took my first bite of the pink slab of meat in front of me. It was fantastic. I welcomed the quiet that came when the band stopped playing and packed up for the night. That was before I spotted her across the room.

She was a solid black cat with big green eyes and in peak athletic condition. She wore a long black silk dress, a gold band around each paw, and the best part was right there around her neck: a gorgeous collar generously adorned in red rubies. Her eyes met mine. I was careless and let my gaze linger just a few seconds too long. She shot me a smile. I had to smile back and throw in a wave for good measure. I turned my attention back to my drink and hoped that would be enough to give me an opportunity to regroup and think of another—

"This seat taken?"

And there she was. Standing just a couple of feet from me with her paw on the back of the empty chair. I smiled.

"Please," I said, gesturing for her to sit down.

"I noticed you looking at me from across the room. I don't normally get that kind of attention from dogs. Not usually from someone so ruggedly handsome either. Most of the boys around here sport that baby face around me if you know what I mean."

"I'm afraid you got it all wrong," I replied.

"Okay. So I've got it all wrong. What were you looking at, then?"

What I wouldn't give to be a fly on the wall that day at the Rose Garden Estates, so I could know if the cat talking to me now was the same cat from back then. Still, this was almost certainly Lily's collar. I had to keep playing the game for now. I guess the real question was whether this was a game being played by Bad Kitty, or if this was some innocent dame who just happened to buy the necklace. "Okay, you got me. You embarrassed me a little coming over here is all. A little more forward than I was expecting from a lady such as yourself."

"You got a name?"

"Trigger."

"Pleasure to meet you, Trigger. I'm Sugarplum. I get the feeling we'll be seeing a lot more of each other." She smiled.

"I'm counting on it." I turned around and called for the bartender. "Another milk for me. Make that two actually. One for the lady here."

He looked at me puzzled. "Lady?"

I thought my problem was keeping my eyes on her too long, but I guess I didn't keep my eyes on her long enough. There was nothing but an empty chair staring back at me when I turned around. I jumped up and ran out of the bar looking in every direction. I'd let her get away. Somehow, though, I was sure she would make good on what she said. We'd be seeing more of each other.

27

I asked the bouncers outside to guess what hotel a super-rich kid like me was staying in. They both guessed the Cloud Nine Hotel, so that's where I went. Asked for the best room in the whole place. Can't go wrong for a hundred bucks a night. It included a private indoor pool, room service, a spa, daily massages, and unlimited meals and snacks on call. The radio was the niftiest thing I'd ever seen. Could operate it on the wall beside the bed and there were speakers all over the room. The television operated on the same control panel and it was in color. It was huge and also built into the wall. I was tempted to watch one of those fancy Greyhound races but decided on a nice jazz station on the radio as I settled into bed.

The next morning, after I had my breakfast, I got a visitor. A Poodle dame in a hotel uniform, here to give me my massage. She took me to the table and asked me to lie on my stomach. She started behind my ears and then moved to my neck, but she got a lot rougher when she came to my shoulders. Then, somehow, she got even rougher. After I felt a hard slap on my back, I turned around to ask her what the big idea was, only to see a sharply dressed Beagle above me with a grin on his face and the masseuse nowhere to be found.

"Hope you don't mind that I sent the poodle on her way. I'm told I give excellent massages."

"You must give a lot of massages to liars," I snapped back, sitting up on the table.

"They're easy to find in this neck of the woods."

"Yeah. I've noticed."

"So, you figured Marty out yet?"

"What do you mean?"

"Come on, detective. What do you think I mean?"

No mask, and no costume, but it was definitely him.

"Why not just come out and tell me, Rico? You like to turn everything into a game?"

"He's one of Mr. B's lapdogs. He's incognito, keeping an eye on Brutus, and he's taken quite an interest in this reel incident."

It finally clicked for me. "And your plan is to pin this whole thing on him? To create chaos within the ranks, huh?"

"Wrong, detective. I'm not going to pin it on anyone," Rico said with a wide smile. "You are."

"I thought you were going right to the top."

"Have a little faith. A bit of patience wouldn't kill you either. And by the way, I heard you visited one of my establishments earlier tonight. What'd you think? Did you try the strawberries chunks in cold milk? That one is my personal favorite."

"Your establishment? You mean the one you frequent?"

"No, I mean mine. I own it."

"So, you're Rick. This explains quite a bit. How you were always so well connected. How you were always so well informed. How you seemed to know when and where to strike when no one else even considered it. And Mr. B has never suspected you?"

"I couldn't say for certain, but why would he? I pay him a very generous sum, and I've never been late on a payment. I've never insulted or criticized him in public, nor have I done anything that would draw even the slightest bit of his attention. In fact, I'd imagine if I ever cross his mind, he'd think quite highly of me."

Just as I was about to interrogate him more, another thought stopped me in my tracks. "Say... you ever heard of Bad Kitty?"

He burst out laughing. "Bad Kitty!? That's a great villain name. If I weren't a dog, I would've used that one for sure."

"Think she works for Mr. B?"

"How would I know?"

"I don't think we should leave any stones unturned here. She could be important," I said.

"Fair point. I'll look into it."

28

I headed back to the Starlight and asked to speak to Mr. Brutus in his office. I filled him in on what happened with his maintenance guy, Brownie, but he didn't seem particularly interested. He asked me if I'd seen the paper this morning. Usually I would've read it by now, but today I hadn't. He slid the paper across his desk in front of me. Right smack in the center of the front page was a picture of Colonel Bones and, of course, yours truly.

I read the entire article. Didn't even ask my permission to have my face printed. Rude. Just the ethics and journalistic integrity one might expect from the *Arc Daily Tribune*. Most of the article droned on and on about the harsh punishments each of the culprits would receive and it ended with a few generic tidbits about how crime doesn't pay. Not even a hint of irony. Unless my own eyes... well, my one eye, was lying to me, crime paid just fine.

"Had quite a busy day yesterday, eh Trigger?"

"I fully expect today to be just as busy."

"Since it looks like I hired the right dog for the job, I'll ignore that little hotel splurge of yours last night. Oh, and how did you enjoy Cloud Nine? I've been there a few times myself. It's quite nice."

"Don't worry. I'll make sure you get your money's worth. And that place was something else. A real treat compared to what I usually sleep in."

"Good," he grunted. "So, what's your next move?"

"Mr. Brutus, have you noticed that Marty seems to take an intense interest in this case?"

"Yes. Is that bad?"

"Perhaps a little more than you'd expect, given his role."

"Why are you asking?"

"Mr. Brutus, how long has he been working for you?"

"A few months now."

"Just enough time to get familiar with the goings on in a place like this. When things arrive and from where. Who does what, and when they hand it off to someone else. You see where I'm going with this?"

"You mean to say he's your number one suspect now, detective?"

"That's right."

"I appreciate you coming to see me first."

"Right. I want you to be present during my interview with Marty. If it's just the two of us, I suspect one of two things will happen. Either you'll get a different side of the story and it'll be my word against his, or he may take a more direct approach. One thing I've noticed about Marty is that he has quite the temper."

His face lit up a little. "No need to concern yourself

with that temper. Why, just a short while ago I was the boxing champion of my weight class here in Adria. It's how I started this business. He may be a big dog, but I think we'll be all right between the two of us." He gave me a wink. "I'll have him brought in."

"Wait just a minute now! You're Brutus the Brute?"

"I see you've heard of me."

"I thought I recognized you from somewhere when I met you. You're Iron Gloves champion Brutus the Brute?"

"That's right," he said proudly.

"I'm a big fan of yours, sir. Used to go to any dive joint with a television and watch your fights. I still remember that fight you had with Little Lou. The one where you won your first title."

"Lou was anything but little. Hit like a Great Dane, he did. Maybe I should take you by the trophy room sometime."

"That would be great, Mr. Brutus."

When Marty came into the office, I carefully positioned myself between him and the door. Thankfully, he didn't seem to expect anything out of the ordinary before he came inside. I felt a little sorry about all this, but only a little. I was sure Marty didn't really commit the crime. No, let's not call it a crime. Let's call it a service. Switching out those reels deserved a big fat medal, though I suspect it was an honor Marty would rather not receive. Thankfully, whoever really swapped out the reels would get off free and having a scumbag like Marty take the fall for it was just icing on the cake as far as I was concerned.

"Have a seat, Marty. I'd like to ask you a few questions."

29

His relaxed smile vanished quickly, and he made a subtle glance toward the door. Poor Marty just had the worst poker face. "You gotta be joking. Do you honestly think I did this?"

"Funny how that's the first thing everyone says, Marty. It's why we have these little question-and-answer sessions. Just to clear the air. Make everyone more comfortable."

He laughed. "You get your picture on the front of the paper and now you think you're top dog. I don't know what you think you know or who you think you're messing with, kid. You're flirting with a whole heap of trouble in this city if you don't play your cards right. You play them right, though, and I think you've got a real future here." He points to the newspaper. "Looks like Colonel Bones was impressed with how you cracked that slot machine rigging operation."

"That a threat or your idea of a bribe?"

"Call it a fortune-telling service, detective. Free of charge."

"You must not be very good at it then."

Watching his grin fade only gave rise to mine.

"At the moment, Marty, I'm more concerned with the past than the future. Tell me, why did you do it?"

"You don't know what you're about to get yourself into."

"Just answer his question, Marty," Brutus said, hoping to defuse the situation. "What harm could there be in playing along? No need to make all these vague threats."

"All right, I'll play along. I didn't do it. Understand? Now, find someone else to bother." He started to walk out.

"Interview's over when I say it's over, Marty."

"It's over, little dog. Know when to quit." He grabbed me and tried to push me aside. Took all I had to slap his paw off my shoulder. A Rottweiler against a Chihuahua wasn't a good matchup. For me.

Brutus jumped up from his desk and made his way over. As Marty reached for the handle, I sank my teeth in his paw. He quickly repaid it by knocking me against the wall, clear across the room. He reached for the handle again and opened the door, but Brutus used his weight to push it shut. Marty took a swing at Brutus, and he took it on the chin. Stood like an oak tree, despite being half his size. He returned a shot of his own to Marty's jaw that sent him on a quick trip to the floor.

I picked myself up and went over to check on Brutus's handiwork. Marty was out cold. I felt lucky to witness a Brutus the Brute knockout firsthand. Something worth bragging about for sure. Good thing he was there, or I'd have been in some real trouble. Marty would have tossed me around like an old rag.

"Good shot, sir. Didn't stand a chance. I'll bet if the police check his apartment, they'll find some evidence."

"I'll call them and have them send a few officers here, along with a couple to meet you at Marty's apartment. You better get going."

He gave me the address and I was on my way.

By the time I got there, a couple of boys in blue were already there waiting for me. Bones was there too. I shouldn't have been surprised.

"We keep running into each other, Trigger. That's good. You've been making my job a lot more interesting these past few days. We were just about to kick in the door and have a look around. Care to join us?"

"I'd love to, Colonel."

He gave his men the word and they knocked the door wide open. Bones and I walked in and turned the place upside down. I missed how easy this used to be when I was on the force. Get a warrant and then kick in doors and flip tables until you found what you were looking for. Super easy and super legal. Nowadays, when I do this sort of thing as a private detective, I have to be sneaky and quiet. And it's not exactly legal.

We found a box pushed under the bed and pulled it out. We ripped open the top and, sure enough, right there with labels and all were the original reels. Now that was something else. There just wasn't any getting out of this. Bones gave me a big pat on the shoulder and we walked out. The press was waiting, snapping pictures as we exited. Bones gave them an interview and pulled me in for a photo op. I wasn't under the impression that turning it down was an option, so I didn't try. I showed them my pearly whites and gave them my best smile. I turned to leave after everyone got their fill.

"Stop by around lunchtime and see me tomorrow at my office," Bones said.

I turned around to see who Bones was talking to; it was me.

"Sir?"

"Can you make it?"

"Well, sure. I can make it."

"Good, see you then."

What had I just gotten myself into?

30

I rang up Brutus to tell him the good news. He said Marty had already been picked up and taken for a quick stop by the hospital. He had to get his jaw wired before heading to the station to get booked. Couldn't have happened to a nicer dog.

Brutus also said he would reopen his theater since Mr. B now accepted the fact that he wasn't responsible, and he told me it would be alright if I spent another night at the hotel on the theater's dime. He'd have the money for completing the case deposited into my account.

I headed back to the hotel to get some sleep, but I took a dip in the hot tub first while having a nice T-bone to top it off. When room service brought my dinner, there were two steaks on the tray. I asked her what the big idea was and if she was trying to make me fat. She said another gentleman would join me for dinner in my room. As is his style, Rick was already waiting for me there, again sporting his suit rather than the ridiculous bandit getup. I put our tray down on the table and joined him.

"Did everything go according to plan, Rick?"

"I think you give me more credit than I deserve here, detective. Everything went a lot better than I had planned. Those dogs and cats rigging the slot machines, for example. Had no idea!"

"So, did you get your guy then?"

"While Marty definitely has a little clout in the organization, he's small fries compared to who we're really after."

"What really needs to change first is the police here. They're more crooked than most of the criminals."

His smile brightened, if such a thing was even possible. "Then you'll really like the second half of our plan."

"I somehow doubt that. Spill it."

"It goes something like this: tomorrow you'll read the paper. If I'm right, you'll see a big print up on the front page featuring you and Colonel Bones. Bones loves that kind of thing. Makes him look great to Mr. B. And because he likes the attention so much, he also likes you. He thinks you're leaving tomorrow. Did he ask you to stop by and see him before you did?"

"In fact, he did. I'm pretty sure I see where this is going and I don't like it."

"He'll ask you to rejoin the force tomorrow, and most likely at your previous rank. You'll agree. You'll do it and play along until a plan or opportunity presents itself to expose Bones and his cops in some huge way they can't easily cover up. Mr. B really depends on the public thinking the police is on their side. A lot of us already know better, but it might surprise you how many have no clue this is happening. Bones works closely with the

Chief of Police. If we can blow the cover on Bones, we can also jeopardize the chief's position. You worked there for a time. I'm sure you still know a few good cops, and a good cop in the position of chief would make all the difference."

"The answer is no," I replied.

"No?"

"That's right. No. I turned down a good cop's offer to join back up with the force in Blue District. So, why would I join up with some corrupt puppet here? Besides, I was on the inside when things were already bad. Do you know the kinds of things I'll probably have to do in order not to blow my cover? The chief will most certainly remember me as well. He'll want me tested to see if I've really changed. He'll expect me to do some terrible things to good dogs and cats, and that crosses a line for me. Would you be willing to do it?"

His smile disappeared in a flash. "I would do whatever it took." He leaned in close, locking eyes with me. "You understand that, detective? Whatever it took."

I got the feeling Rick had more at stake here than I initially thought. This wasn't just a game to him. Well, it wasn't just a game to me either. I stood up, our eyes still locked. "The answer is no. Pay me whatever you think is fair and find someone else to be your stooge. Now if you'll be so kind as to leave me in peace while I enjoy my steak."

"Trigger, you're making a big mistake. You have a chance to do some real good here. The kind of good you may never have the chance to do again. You're a brilliant detective. Do you really want to spend the rest of your life helping grandmas find their lost house keys for pocket change? So you don't want to make any powerful enemies anymore. I get that, but let me tell you one thing. The number of bad people you have for enemies is directly proportional to the number of good deeds you've done. The more powerful those enemies are, the more powerful a force of good you are. Are you really going to put your own selfish feel-good morals above the lives of the many people who live here? Or is it that you've just become a coward?"

I flipped the table to the side, with steaks and plates and cutlery crashing to the floor. "Get out!" I screamed.

He stood up and walked slowly toward the door. He stopped just before leaving, hesitating before speaking. "Just give it some thought."

31

I tossed and turned in my sleep, finding that no rest or comfort would come. But that dream came back again. The nightmare, to be more specific. It was a day I'd never forget.

"Let it go, Lieutenant. If you go through with this, it'll be your badge."

"Buzz off, Patches. Go lick the chief's boots some more. It's what you're good at."

"You don't get it, Trigger. When you're making omelets, you gotta break some eggs. I know how you feel, but you have to let this one go, pal."

"We ain't pals, and I said buzz off. He beat that poor dame half to death just for turning him down and throwing in a few insults. I don't give a rat's tail that he's the mayor's pup, Patches. I don't care if he's the mayor himself. Nobody's above the law."

"If you do this, Trigger, then any chance you had of changing anything within the department is gone. It's over. It'll be a long time before this blows over, even if you somehow manage to keep the badge. The chief will never trust you with authority again. You're a lieutenant, and high on the list to make colonel. If you keep your nose clean in the department, you'll be ready to make a grab for chief the first opportunity something happens. Imagine what you could do then."

"Yeah? And what's it worth if I have to be just as bad as the chief to get there? You think this dame will remember what happened and be grateful we sat on our tails and played the long game?"

He didn't answer. He looked down at his feet, trying to find the words to make his point, but I interrupted the process.

"Get out of my way. If you've not made any enemies, then you've never done the right thing when it mattered. So long, Patches. Good luck on the inside."

I walked past him and into the next room where several officers had heard what I was planning to do. They were waiting, ready to follow me. I said a few words about how the law must apply to all equally, or it wasn't the law at all. To my surprise, the room erupted in thunderous applause. After that, we set out for the mayor's son's house.

We were told we weren't allowed back into Capitol District until this whole charade blew over, but the news hadn't spread yet. It might've also been the fact that we looked imposing marching down the street the way we did. Maybe the Capitol District police knew they were supposed to stop us but didn't. Maybe they agreed with what we stood for and didn't want to get in the way.

I knocked on his door.

"Police! Open up!"

A young Collie came to the door. "Sure, I don't remember

inviting you to the party, but come on in. Just behave while you're here or dad won't be happy."

He was confident that nothing would happen to him. So self-assured he didn't even consider why we were there. The chief was such buddies with the mayor and Mr. B that he assumed we were actually there to party with him.

I signaled for my boys to come inside with me. I followed him to his chair in the back of the room which he'd fashioned to look like a throne. Music was playing; the room was full of young somebodies having a good time.

"Turn off the music."

"What? Why?"

I pointed to one of my officers, then to the radio. "Turn it off." He walked over and switched off the music.

"Who do you think you are?"

"I'm Lieutenant Trigger of the ACPD. Are you Jimmy?"

"I prefer to be called Jimmy Jim. It's what all my friends call me." He laughs, and all the other somebodies laugh on cue.

"Jimmy Jim." I smiled. "You're under arrest for felony aggravated assault."

He stood up, a big grin on his face. "Sorry, Lieutenant. You and your men must have some outdated information."

"Come quietly, or I'll have to embarrass you in front of your fancy friends here, but given the grins on their faces, maybe that's something they would like to see."

He lashed out, screaming at me so hard I could feel his spittle hitting me on the face. "You wait until my father-"

I took my open paw and slapped him across the face. The room went silent and grins turned to frowns. He looked as if he was about to sob, his bottom lip quivering.

"Don't let me interrupt, Jimmy Jim. You were saying?"

He half-turned his head away while still looking at me, a tear falling down his cheek. His lip was still quivering and he said nothing.

"Come on, tough guy. Finish what you were about to say. Something about your father. What? Cat got your tongue?"

Again, he stood silent, trembling.

I motioned to the officer closest. "Cuff him. Hopefully he'll resist. If he does, make sure to use whatever force you deem necessary."

Jimmy didn't resist. We walked him all the way back through Capitol District with a raucous audience most of the way.

As soon as we got to the station, Jimmy was promptly released and given a personal apology from the chief, and I was "asked" to hand in my badge. Patches made a case for the other boys, saying they were just following orders (like I should've been), so they got off with a slap on the paw. One of the hardest lessons I ever learned with the ACPD was what it meant to be real *police.*

I woke up in a cold sweat a lot earlier than I had intended, but I knew there'd be no going back to sleep. Rick's words kept buzzing around in my head. In the time that had passed, it seemed I wasn't as sure of myself anymore on the right or wrong answer. I think it was probably because there was no right or wrong answer. Maybe it was time to try things their way.

32

I walked down to the Adria police precinct and told the receptionist I was there to see Bones. This place looked more like the headquarters of a bank too big to fail than a police station; waxed tile floors, fancy lights lining the top edge of the wall, big windows everywhere, spiraling metal staircases, and, of course, the giant token fountain in the middle of the lobby. What a joke.

The receptionist showed me to his office. It made Brutus's office look like mine by comparison. There was a mini golf setup and all. Next I would probably see the top dogs light their cigars with hundred-dollar bills. Made sense, though. The police here were essential to Mr. B and making his operation run smoothly. Maybe they were even more critical to Mr. B's enterprise than I initially thought.

"Trigger, glad you could make it," Bones said, waving me in.

"Nice office you've got here," I replied.

"You like it? There's one almost as nice as this empty down the hall."

"You don't say?"

"You know, I heard about that little stunt you pulled a while back over in the Capitol District."

"Oh yeah?"

"Yeah. I don't really care, but the chief's got a long memory. You hear me?"

I grunted in affirmation.

"You've made me look great to some very important people over the last couple of days. I like that. Mr. B had some nice gifts sent over for me to show his gratitude. I even took it upon myself to have a suit sized for you. I hope you don't mind. I'm usually a good judge of measurements." He held up the suit in front of me before handing it over.

"Don't mind at all. Could use another suit. This'll actually be the nicest set of threads I've ever owned, in fact."

"It's only fair you get something given the role you played. There's a lot more where that came from if you do as you're expected to do. In fact, it's almost a sure bet I'll make chief when that position opens again. That'll leave a nice little opening here," he said.

"Yeah, I suppose the chief's getting up there in years."

"Well, as I'm sure you're aware, old age isn't the only thing that can help the chief find his way out of his position. Disappointing Mr. B is the quickest way to find yourself out of anything. This mortal coil included. What would you say to rejoining the force? The chief advised against it, but since Mr. B has been so pleased with me lately, he's afraid to outright tell me no. You've got a lot of talent and experience, so I wouldn't expect you to come on as just some regular cop and start over. You can come back as a lieutenant. You could be my right-paw dog.

"Keep making me look good and when I'm the chief, you can be Colonel in Adria. To be honest, that position is just about as good. You get to work directly with Mr. B, living as good and easy a life as you could imagine. Like I said before, all you have to do is what you're told and when you're told to do it. That part's not as bad as it sounds. Most dogs and cats here fall in line with very little persuasion. However, occasionally you may need to remind the residents who *really* runs this place in person. Give 'em a little physical persuasion. Nobody holds out forever if you make the right threats and push the right buttons. Everyone has their price, as they say."

"You know, I really am tired of sticking my neck out all the time for folks who don't appreciate it. I tried the straight and narrow. I tried taking a stand and seeing what would change. Then I came to realize that what really needed to change was me. I was one of the best detectives the department ever had. Where did that land me? Slumming it in Black District, barely making enough to cover the bills. I'll take you up on that offer. Sign me up." Bones would have to be more delusional than I thought to buy that mediocre performance, but given his relaxed expression I hit home plate.

"Good. I'm glad to hear it. I want you to keep in mind what I said though. The fastest way to living with regret for the rest of your very short life is to disappoint Mr. B.

For you, disappointing me is basically the same thing. Is that crystal?"

"Yes, sir."

Bones called HQ and had the chief add me to the roster: Lieutenant Trigger. I had to admit that it had a nice ring to it. He issued me a badge and one of those fancy electric batons the police in Adria wielded. I guess this was a smaller version of what those dogs at the gate were using. You press a button, then it makes this awful crackling sound. They say it's enough to deter almost anyone without even having to use it. As per standard procedure, I had to take a hit from it before being officially issued one. As soon as it touched me, every muscle in my body contracted and burned and I toppled over like a little Chihuahua statue. When I came to, we all had a good laugh about it.

Shortly after I'd settled into my new office, a buzz came from the intercom.

"Lieutenant, Colonel Patches would like to speak with you."

"Put him through."

"Lieutenant Trigger speaking."

"Trigger, what do you think you're doing? I saw the roster update. I offered to get you hired back. What's the big idea?"

"Well, it's a lot nicer here in Adria, Colonel."

"What, did you suddenly find yourself attracted to the stink of corruption? I gotta tell you, you may not think what you did with the mayor's son that day did any good. You'd be wrong. People still talk about that here. It gives them hope. They know what a good cop looks like."

"Those boys who work for you, they still do," I replied. "Now, I need to be going if there are no other pressing matters. I have a lot of work to do. Wish me luck."

"You better be on your toes, Trigger. No amount of luck can help you out of the predicament you've gotten yourself in now."

After he hung up, I wondered whether he realized what was really going on. Couldn't be sure, but he sounded angry. I laughed aloud. Guess it didn't really make much difference. Like he said, no amount of luck would get me through this. I'd have to be on my toes.

33

The coming weeks were a real challenge. I realized the Adria police force was mainly a shakedown racket that worked for Mr. B directly. Bones really meant what he said when he explained that I needed to do exactly what I was told to do and exactly when I was told to do it. That's how it worked every day.

A few cats wanted to open a new casino on the far end of Adria. Bones and I went to have a talk with them, just to let them know what the rules would be. See, no one was ever outright denied the opportunity to open a new business, even one that competed with Mr. B. It was just made clear to that individual, or individuals, that a specific cut of the profits would need to be sacrificed as a cost of doing business. It was just another "business expense". They distributed those forfeited profits to the police (a small portion) while the rest went to Mr. B.

We dedicated most of the rest of our time to those who forgot about this arrangement, either by trying to hide their profits or by *forgetting* to make a payment.

That's where folks like Marty came in. You never knew who these dogs or cats were. All you knew is that you thought you were hiding things really well, then suddenly you're getting a visit from the boys in blue reminding you of your overdue payment. Just a friendly reminder at first; however, you didn't want us coming back asking twice. Things got a lot less sympathetic and friendly as the visits increased. You'd get a third visit, and it was something you would really remember. That's because, on this visit, the nice guy routine was over. There wasn't even the courtesy of fake pleasantries. This reminder was the "final notice".

Then came the fourth visit, with you or your business, or both, getting pretty roughed up. If, after this, you were still crazy enough to not pay into the racket, it was easy for us to find a violation. We used it to shut your business down, and that's if you were lucky. If no such violation existed, we made one up. The court to appeal these violations was in Adria, and corrupt to the core. That was that. Real slick operation. No recourse.

I had a real fancy apartment not too far from the station, and I stayed in touch with Rick, although very infrequently. Occasionally he would feed me some information; the names of individuals or businesses to investigate. Sure enough, I would find some minor legal offense to get them on. I already had a knack for investigative work, but I was a real superstar with Rick's help. The whole department was taking notice, and at one point, Mr. B even sent a gift addressed directly to me. It was a gold watch. I had only ever seen a couple like it before; one of which was on the wrist of one Colonel Bones.

There were only a couple of places to get them because no one really bought them, even here. These were the pointless things people would buy just so their friends and associates would know how rich they were. The darn thing told time just like any other watch, except this one cost about a thousand times more.

Rick rang me up one night, telling me about a very interesting target. It was Brutus, owner of the Starlight. It seemed that recently he stopped paying his share to the department, which I suspected Rick had something to do with. We went down and had a talk with him, but with the same result every time. He flat out refused to pay. Said a movie theater ought to be a legitimate business no matter where it was. Said families and kids used that theater. He didn't want gangsters or gangsters pretending to be cops showing up. Oh, that really grabbed Bones's tuft the wrong way. He really didn't think of himself as a gangster. He thought of this as a cost, or a perk, of policing in Adria. Most criminals he didn't let off. In fact, he was harsh toward criminals. That was unless that criminal had a connection to Mr. B. Those were not criminals to Bones, rather business associates. They got a free pass. Talk about twisted logic.

The day before we were to go deliver our fourth warning to Brutus, Rick called and gave me some precise instructions so I could offer them in the form of suggestions to Bones. He told me where to go in, where we would speak to Brutus, and precisely what time the physical part would take place. Someone leaked information to the department that the theater would be closed. However, information was given to other individuals that there was to be a private showing of a play. It would take place in one of the main theater halls. The audience was given strict instructions to remain completely silent, as there would be a special opening planned for the play that would take place behind the curtain. Attendees were told that the actors were sensitive to any noise or reaction from the audience, so it was essential that there be complete silence and lack of movement on part of those attending. The attendees were all the elite performance critics from Adria and beyond. In fact, every district was to be represented in the audience. Critics were to sign ironclad nondisclosure agreements; they could inform no one else of their attendance.

Brutus, upon our arrival, was waiting for us exactly where I was told he would be. He was standing out in the hallway where the offices were and we gave chase the moment we saw him. Brutus was a fast runner as it turned out. He had no problem staying just ahead of us the entire way. We went through rehearsal rooms and found ourselves finally backstage, then we went onto the stage behind the curtain. There was complete silence. I knew what was about to happen, but no one else did. I assumed that Brutus did too, but even that I didn't know for sure.

When Brutus was cornered on the stage, he turned to us and shouted.

"You're the true criminals of this city, the lot of you! A scourge on the good people of this district who work hard just so you can play henchmen for Mr. B."

Bones never passed up an opportunity to get on his

soapbox. He was quick to point out the specifics of the arrangement.

"Brutus, you act as if this is all unreasonable and without warning. You needed only to pay the protection fee to Mr. B. Then none of this would be happening right now. You've been paying it fine until now. I've seen your books. It's only a small portion of your profits, so you're more than capable of doing it. You have no one to blame for this but yourself!"

"I'll not try to reason further with thugs who treat the uniform as a mere costume that makes it easier to shake-down citizens."

We surrounded Brutus, and, despite how good of a scrapper he was, we gave him a sound beating. He delivered a compelling shot to my jaw. If this was a performance, it sure felt authentic, even though I knew it wasn't on account of what I saw him do to Marty. What a guy.

The curtain opened just as Bones was about to get his feel. The look on everyone's face was that of pure horror, including the faces of the police who just got caught red-handed doing a shakedown for Mr. B's protection racket. The audience had heard everything and now they'd seen it too. Bones ordered everyone to stay put, but that didn't even come close to happening. Before he even got the sentence out, half the audience had jumped up and ran out. It was too dark to see who they were or to even get a good look at their faces. We were up on stage and it was well lit. Everyone saw all of our faces, and clearly.

34

All we could do was sit tight and wait. The next morning, we went into the department as usual, and it didn't take long to notice that the phone wasn't ringing. Bones was bouncing his foot excessively under his desk. The toothy, forced smile showed me he was attempting to hold on to the confidence that everything would work out. He seemed sure that no matter what happened, no matter what kind of trouble he found himself in, that Mr. B would get him out of it. He was probably right. But that didn't mean things couldn't get interesting anyway.

I heard a commotion coming from outside. It was a few dozen officers from the Blue District approaching. Marching right at the front was Colonel Patches himself. I could barely contain my excitement, which thankfully looked enough like fear that no one seemed to notice. One of the Adria officers met them at the door and told them they weren't allowed inside and that they didn't have jurisdiction here. He was promptly ignored and shoved aside, landing flat on the floor. I and several others ran straight to Colonel Bones's office, though I went there for a different reason than everyone else. It took just a few seconds for Patches to make his way up the steps and into the office, where he met Bones face-to-face. Bones had stood in front of his desk, paws behind his back, waiting.

"Patches, just what do you think you're doing here?"

"Isn't it obvious, Bones?"

"What's obvious, Colonel, is that you don't have jurisdiction here. You are about to make a big mistake."

"No, you're the one who made a mistake. You broke the law, and there are enough witnesses that even you won't be able to get out of it this time."

"So what? So I committed a crime, and a bunch of folks saw me. I'm sure you're aware of who I work for. Both officially and unofficially. Either of which can put you in your place and make sure this is something you will come to sorely regret. You sure you want to go down this path?"

"Mr. B hasn't so much as sent his lowest crony to your defense. It seems that your gross incompetence has left him feeling a little disappointed."

Bones's smile slowly faded from his face. He understood almost immediately that this part was definitely true. After all, he'd just warned me of the same thing recently. You will undoubtedly regret it if you disappoint Mr. B.

"You listen here, small fry. You wait until I call the chief and—"

"Call him," Patches said as he pointed to the phone on the desk. "Let's find out what he has to say."

Was that sweat pouring down his cheeks?

"Fine," Bones spat. "Let's see how much of a big shot you are after the chief hears about this."

Bones set the phone to speaker and dialed. "ACPD, how may I direct your call?" the voice said.

"Put me through to the Chief of Police! I need to talk to him, now!" Bones demanded.

"Sir, I'm very sorry. The chief isn't available right now."

"What do you mean he isn't available right now? Do you know who I am? This is Colonel Bones. If you know what's good for you, you'll put me through to the chief's office right this second."

"It's not that I don't want to put you through to the chief's office, Colonel. It's just that the chief's not in right now. They arrested the previous chief this morning, and the new chief left a little while ago. In fact, now that I think of it, he said he was on his way to see you. He should be there any minute, so you can talk to him in person."

Bones' erratic arm gestures quickly turned into slumped shoulders. His paw was shaking as he reached over to hang up the call. He stood up straight, looking in Patches' direction, but his eyes seemed to go right through him. Patches reached into his jacket pocket and pulled out his badge, holding it out for Bones to read. There, right across the top and bottom, the badge stated in raised, bold lettering: ARC CITY CHIEF OF POLICE.

"Colonel Bones, I hereby relieve you of duty. You and your entire department are under arrest for corruption and racketeering. You'll be coming with me quietly.

Personnel from Blue District will run your department until we can sift through the weeds." The smile stretching across Patches' face was brighter than the sun.

I wanted to cheer. I wanted to clap. Unfortunately, I also wanted to keep my cover for just a bit longer. Wanted to save my own neck, to be precise. I would have to settle for all that happening in my head and celebrating on the inside. Bones offered his paws up for cuffing without a fight while the other officers and I followed suit. They arrested every officer in the department.

A series of trials took place over the coming weeks, and Mr. B made it very clear how he felt about the entire thing. He did precisely nothing. He sent none of his goons to interfere with the trial. No one was visited in the dark of night, or during the day for that matter. The Chief of Police... former Chief, I should say, was convicted and sent to prison. Bones and the rest of the department of Adria sat in prison awaiting their own trials. This was along with many officers in other districts who had served the former chief a little too faithfully. I, on the other hand, had received a quiet pardon after Patches identified me as a confidential informant. Seems Rick was secretly sending the information to Patches with my name on it. Not that I'm complaining. Rick didn't want to be identified, and I was happy having my hide saved.

I was finally back in the Black District, and happy to be there. Back in my little office, far away from all the lights and excitement. I would have been happy if it stayed that way, but nothing ever works out the way you want it to in this city.

35

In the coming weeks, things really improved in the city. No criminal was safe anymore with Patches at the helm. Arrests were happening one after another, the jails were running out of space, the courts were getting backed up, and the best part of all was that crime went down. It really went down for the first time in a long time. Folks were feeling safer in their own homes.

Remember how I said things never go the way you want for long? Well, they didn't.

A buzz startled me as I sat in my chair struggling to read the newspaper under my desk lamp. Jumped so hard I almost knocked the thing over. Piece of junk burned hot enough to bake a pizza under it, so I couldn't stand to have it on more than a few minutes at a time. Should've replaced it ages ago.

"Detective, there is a nicely dressed dog and cat here to see you," Zelda said.

"They been here before?" I asked.

"No, they've never been here before. He said this visit

was a long time coming, so I thought you might be expecting them."

"Go ahead and send—" I suddenly got a sinking feeling in my stomach. Something wasn't right. This visit was a long time coming? Sounded like these two thought maybe *I* had it coming. I'd given Zelda a code phrase for just this situation. It let her know to calmly get out and get help. "Say, it's been a long day. Why don't you head on home after you send them in? Don't worry, I'll lock up when I'm done, *but don't forget to lock the box on the way out.*"

"Okay, Trigger. I'll see you tomorrow," she said calmly.

I recognized immediately who the dog was as the two visitors came in, which made my heart skip a few beats. It was Marty. I'd never seen the cat with him. He was a big orange tabby wearing a suit that looked like it cost more than the real estate in this whole district. Marty pulled out a chair in front of my desk for him. No way... Was this who I thought it was? If I was to have any hope of making it out of here alive, I really hoped it wasn't. Just on the small chance I hadn't been found out, I played it cool.

"Have a seat, gentlemen." I motioned to the two chairs in front of me. They were both so calm I was really starting to hope they were here for reasons other than what I suspected. Marty spoke first.

"It's good to see you again, detective. I finally got that wire taken out of my jaw. See?" He rubbed his jaw with his paw.

I offered my best smile. "Good for you, Marty. I'm glad you could get out of that whole mess, but I figured you would. I'm sure you noticed that... after that happened, I joined up with Bones to do a lot of good for Mr. B in Adria. Well, that was until Bones dropped the ball. He really messed up the whole plan. I had no choice but to come back here and lie low for a while. When things blow over, I could come back and get things going again."

I kept waiting for that big orange cat to speak, but he wouldn't. He just kept smiling at me. No matter what I said, all he would do is that menacing thin smile. The anticipation was killing me, but I couldn't just outright ask. If he was worth knowing, I'd find out soon enough.

"Yeah? That's so good to hear. You know, me and my friend here were curious how you avoided going to jail with Bones and all the others, so we thought we'd come down here in person and ask."

"Well, you see, I spilled my guts at the last minute. Made a deal with Patches that would get me off. I had to sell out a few of the small fries to do it, but I'm sure you could understand why I did it." The two of them looked at each other. The big orange cat still smiling like he had from the moment he walked into the room, except now Marty was smiling too. They both laughed like I had just told the world's funniest joke without meaning to. The big orange cat stood up.

"I've wanted to meet you for a long time, detective. And I must admit, you did not disappoint. It really is a shame we know absolutely everything there is to know about you. We know that you were working for someone to disrupt my operations in Adria. We don't know who it was yet, but we will soon. After today, I think you will find that they will be sufficiently provoked into exposing themselves. I'm sorry, I misspoke. After today you won't be finding much of anything unless it's at the bottom of the Adria River." He turned to leave the room, just as Marty rubbed his right fist into his left paw.

"What's your name, cat? At least tell me your name!"

"My name? Vash is my name." He turned to walk away but stopped at the door. He turned back around and gave me that big bright smile again. "Oh, excuse me. You probably know me as Mr. B. It was a pleasure meeting you, detective. A shame that this will only be our first and last meeting. So long. Marty, do what you came here to do and be done with it. I'll meet you back in Adria."

36

I knew the chances of me getting out of this alive were close to zero - on a good day. I considered what I had done in my life and whether it was good enough. With the last few weeks taken into consideration, I decided that it would just have to be. I thought about Lily, Sugarplum, and all the other unfinished work. Shame I wouldn't get to close the case.

Marty and I sat there looking at each other for several minutes after Vash, aka Mr. B, had left. Seemed that as loyal as he was, he was still intent to toy with me, even if Mr. B had asked him not to. Marty enjoyed seeing me tremble and he would savor every second of it. While keeping my eyes on him, I slipped a letter opener out of a slight crack in my desk drawer and into my right paw. Marty was far beyond my weight class, so if I wanted to have even the tiniest chance of making it out with my breathing privileges still intact, I had to surprise him by acting first.

As soon as he stood up, I kicked my desk forward, right into him. The impact caused him to fall onto it and catch himself with his left paw. The moment his paw touched the desk, I jumped up and slammed the letter opener into his paw, pinning it to the desk. I wasted no time throwing several punches into his face, hopefully right where his jaw was broken recently. I nailed it. With a satisfying crack, I could hear Marty's jaw break once again under my fist. After about three good punches, he pulled the letter opener out of his paw and hit me hard enough to send me flying against the back wall. I slammed against it so hard that my framed Rose Garden Estates ticket came crashing down, littering the surrounding floor with shattered glass. Seemed the pain just made him angrier.

He made his way over and picked me up by the scruff of my neck. I picked up a shard of the broken glass and stabbed it into his right forearm, which left both of us with nasty cuts. He dropped me, and when I landed on my feet I threw several more punches square into his gut. The effect was small, but it was something. He kicked me. I went sailing across the room again and into the other wall. I felt several of my ribs break. Even though I was doing better than I had any right to be, it still wasn't going well. He approached me again, but this time I lunged toward him and sank my teeth into his paw. I felt small bones crack. He tried to shake me loose, but I held on and kept biting as hard as I could, the metallic taste of blood filling my mouth. He picked me up off the ground and carried me over to my desk, where he slammed my head repeatedly onto the top of it before dragging me across, knocking everything off onto the floor. My vision clouded like I was trying to wake up from a bad dream. If I passed out it would be over for me.

As I was about to go over the other end of the desk, I grabbed the handle of my drawer. I pulled it out with me as I sailed across the room. Its contents littered the floor, but luck was on my side. Marty saw me reaching for the electric baton on the floor and reacted quickly, trying to stop me. He ran over and gave me a swift kick to the head. My nose felt like it broke in fifty different places, but when I hit the wall for the third time, I was relieved to find I had somehow kept hold of the baton.

He came over and grabbed me around the neck, picking me up and slamming me against the wall. His face told me everything. It was the face of an assassin, intent on finishing the job. I struggled to find the switch on the baton as he was choking the life out of me. I found it, just as I felt as if I would pass out. I pressed the baton against his rib cage and turned it on. As the device crackled to life, he dropped me to the floor and I gasped for breath, grabbing every ounce of sweet, cold air I could. As we both struggled to get to our feet, I made it to my feet first, delivering two solid blows to his head with the baton. I didn't have the strength in me to stay standing, much less hit him again.

That all changed when I looked over and realized the lamp I had on my desk was now on the floor, broken and resting on the rapidly igniting paper. It was lighting the place up quick. I used every last ounce of the strength I had left to drag myself out of the back door and into the alley behind my office. I wasn't sure if I would ever wake up again, but I was dead tired. I turned to take one last look at my office as the fire consumed every square inch of it. It seemed like I couldn't wake up from the nightmare after all.

37

I woke up in a hospital bed, and I may as well have been opening my eyes into the sun itself. It would be nice if these white rooms weren't as familiar, but unfortunately I had been in a few too many of them throughout my life. As I rolled over, I realized I had company at my bedside. One Lieutenant Buddy.

"Look who finally decided nap time was over," Buddy said, smugly.

"I didn't realize you cared so much, Buddy."

"Yeah, me and about a dozen other boys the chief has secretly spread around the building."

Suddenly it hit me. I remembered what happened leading up to where I blacked out. "My office?" Buddy frowned and shook his head slowly. "What about Marty? He make it out?"

"Yeah, he made it. You know, the boys downtown had quite a laugh after hearing about what went down. Never seen a Rottweiler licked so hard by a Chihuahua before. He was in the same hospital until just this morning," Buddy explained. "But don't worry, he's enjoying a very secure cell right now. No one's springing him this time."

"So how long have I been in here?"

"Only a few days. Well... technically you're dead."

"Dead?"

"The chief thought it would be a good idea. Give you a chance to lie low for a while and recover. See for yourself." He tossed the newspaper on my bed and I immediately flipped through the pages, making my way to the obituaries. Sure enough, there I was. It was quite an exciting thing to see. I bet not many dogs live to be old enough to see their own obituary. And that wasn't the only interesting thing I saw in the paper. Many of the white-collar criminals Patches had arrested were being found not guilty at the trials, despite overwhelming evidence against them. It appeared that Mr. B still had full control where he wanted it. Those who failed him he was happy to let go, and when he wanted you out, you were out. It looked like the department would once again find its paws tied.

"I need to speak to him," I said.

"Do you know how busy the chief is right now? Is this not something you could just tell me?"

"Sure. I could tell you. And you'll tell me we need to take this information to the chief."

Buddy laughed. "Try me."

"You want to know who paid me a visit?"

"Yeah, Marty. We've already been over this."

"He didn't come visit me by himself. He had a tag-along who left before the fun started."

Buddy looked vaguely disinterested when his eyebrows furrowed. "I'm all ears."

"A big, fat orange cat by the name of Vash."

"Vash?"

"Yeah, that's his real name. At least, that's the name he gave me. No reason to think he lied, considering he was certain I would be worm food in the coming minutes. No harm in telling your real name to a dead dog."

"Whose real name?"

I sighed. "Mr. B."

His eyes bulged. "Mr. B?! *The* Mr. B? I'm sure you're well aware that Mr. B isn't known for his meet and greets."

"No kidding. Lucky me. I must've really gotten under his hide."

"Well, you were right about one thing. We need to take this information to the chief. I'm sure he'll be back to see you shortly. By the way, your name is Carson. You're an insurance investigator. Mr. B needs to think Marty finished the job for as long as possible. It'll give you some breathing room." He handed me a fake ID. Decently made, but not enough to convince anyone who gave it a closer look.

"Carson. Got it."

Patches came into the room a few hours later, and I brought him up to speed on everything. He told me about the plan he'd come up with to fake my death. It turned out that Zelda, that forgetful old dog, did in fact remember my warning phrase and alerted the police as soon as she left the building. They got there just in time to drag Marty out the back, but not enough time to save the building. Things would've been a lot easier if I hadn't had my face plastered all over the paper in Adria several times over, but at least there had been no good close-ups that would give away my bad eye. I still had to be careful who I asked questions around and make sure the wrong people didn't get a good look at my face. The fact that I had one eye would be a problem. The chief had me discharged and gave me directions to a safe house here in the Black District. I took my papers and promptly made my way toward Adria. The chief would be livid, but probably not surprised. Carson, the insurance investigator, had things to do.

38

Before I got there, I made a stop at the residence of an old friend; reformed forger by the name of Harvey. Harvey was a beagle who got mixed up with the wrong dogs when he was just a pup. He tried to leave the business early on, but those he worked for don't take kindly to early retirement. The dog had a real talent for forgeries. I busted up the whole operation and let Harvey escape during the raid. When it came time to testify, I seemed to forget he was there or even involved. How weird is that?

Harvey was a good kid. I knew a bad apple when I saw one, and he was as far away from that as they come. Folks needed to live in the Black District for a while to understand how good dogs and cats get forced into these operations, then end up in jail with the rest. I just couldn't abide by that.

He was reluctant, but he put together some real quality products. I needed convincing documentation "proving" my occupation in the event someone pressed me for it. If I'd have investigated Carson myself, I wouldn't have given it a second thought. I thanked him for his work and made one more stop to pick up a fresh suit.

I opted for something low key, but Adria low key. I couldn't be looking like I was a cop, but often the insurance investigators I met were snazzier dressed and just as mean. Meaner, actually. At least it wasn't a stretch for me. I picked the blue pinstripe I could afford with the twenty in my pocket and added the matching hat. The widest brimmed fedora they had with the front folded down a tad. It would do wonders for my short stature, hopefully hiding the eyes without looking too out of sorts. Unfortunately for me, a one-eyed Chihuahua was easier to pick out of a crowd than the two-eyed variety.

I had no trouble at the gate. I waited for a crowd, flashed my pass, and walked right in like I owned the place. I had a good handle on where I wanted to go, but I'd shown up to the commercial hub of the city with just a few dollars in my pocket. I had good money in my bank account, but I couldn't exactly walk into a bank and inform the teller that a dead dog was here to make a withdrawal. I would need help and in more ways than one. I made my way straight to Rick's corporate headquarters.

I asked the secretary at the front desk to see him.

"Got an appointment?" the secretary blurted out.

"I don't need one. Tell him an investigator is here to see him. He'll-"

"I don't care who you are. Come back when you have an appointment," she replied.

"It's urgent, ma'am. I need to see him right away. It's-"

"You and half of Adria. Now scram."

I started to speak again, but this time she just made a threatening nod toward a very large security dog. I realized quickly that I was going nowhere fast with this tenacious gatekeeper. I'd seen prison wardens easier to crack. I went outside, and after spending several precious minutes wandering around I found a payphone. Using an even more precious quarter I rang his direct line. No answer. Now I had less time, less money, and nothing to show for it. *Great start.*

I had nowhere to stay. I couldn't be caught sleeping in some alley, and as the hour grew late, it looked more and more like an all-nighter. I made my way to the one place I remembered a dog could spend the night awake without drawing suspicion. The ironically named Sweet Dreams.

I made my way there and wove a tall tale at the door about how I was a food critic sent by the paper, eventually getting inside. I went up to the bar, ordered a glass of water, gave the barkeep a nickel, and sat at the first open corner table. I sipped on that water as slow as physically possible. I had a lot of time to pass.

It wasn't long before the waiter came to my table asking me to order more or vacate. At first I told him I was waiting for two friends of mine, also food critics, but after an hour he stopped buying it. I made up excuse after excuse until finally he wasn't having it anymore. He said he'd send his pal over to see me next time.

A few minutes later, a pit bull, looking about as rough and mean as he was big, came over and sat down at the table across from me. He was the most polite dog I'd ever met explaining how he was about to open the exit door with my face, which made me believe him all the more. He stood up and put his paw on my shoulder, at about the same time that a black cat's paw came to rest on his forearm.

"Relax. He's with me."

"Sorry Sugarplum, but I know trouble when I see it. He's gotta go, the bouncer said."

"No problem. I'll just give my father a call. You can sort it out with him."

"No! No, that won't be necessary. Please, enjoy your night."

The slender black cat was a sight for sore eyes, but I found her one part intriguing and one part frightening. But at the moment, she was the closest thing I had to a friend in Adria.

39

"I had a feeling we'd see each other again, Mr.—"

"Carson. Mr. Carson."

"Right, Mr. Carson. Remind me again what you did for a living," Sugarplum purred.

"Insurance investigator, ma'am."

She grinned, looking as though she was holding back a giggle. "Right. Insurance investigator. So, Mr. Carson, you seem to be down on your luck tonight. I've been watching you since you came in here. Either you're hiding out or you've got nowhere to go. I'm desperately curious as to which one it is."

"A little of both, but more of the latter I'm afraid."

"What insurance claim are you investigating, Mr. Carson?"

"An expensive collar, one covered in red jewels. You know, now that I think about it, it's not too dissimilar to the one you wear. In fact, it's basically identical. Seen any others like it around the city?"

"I can't say I have. In fact, I'm fairly certain it's one of a kind," she replied.

"One of a kind, you say?"

"Yes. I'm drawn to the things that no one else can have."

"How do you know the collar is one of a kind? Also, how did you get it?"

"Mr. Carson, let's not waste our time. You know either I'm telling you the truth already, or I won't tell you the truth. Either way, you can't prove that this collar is the one you're looking for. Besides, I'm sure you have bigger fish to fry at the moment."

Unfortunately, she was right. As much as I would've enjoyed grilling her about the collar, she was my one and only benefactor at the moment. Besides, I really did have bigger fish to fry.

"All right, Sugarplum. You win. Maybe let's talk about who I think might have stolen it."

"Oh please, let's do that."

"Does the name Bad Kitty mean anything to you?"

"Bad Kitty? Never heard of a cat by that name. How do you know it wasn't Rico? After all, he's the most successful thief around. Actually, the buzz is that they caught him last night, but they're keeping it out of the papers because daddy wants it that way."

She sent me reeling with two solid verbal punches in one breath. "Now wait just a minute. Caught?"

"Yep, caught. I think it's a real shame, too. I always looked up to him. I liked the way he would get daddy in a big fit."

"Okay, what's this 'daddy' business?"

"Oh, you know who I mean. Normally I keep that on the down low, but I see no point in doing that with you. You'll just find out eventually anyway, and by then you'll be cross at me for hiding it from you. So, there we are, out in the open. Mr. B is my father. Although somewhat estranged," Sugarplum said.

"Just how estranged are we talking?"

"We are not on speaking terms at the moment. See, I wanted to restructure the operation. Turn it into something legitimate before it's too late. He insists on doubling down even though anyone can see how this will end. If not now, then soon. A well-maintained, legitimate company can last for countless generations."

I nodded, unconvinced. "Sure."

"Think about it like this, Mr. Carson. Would you rather make two hundred today or fifty dollars every day for the next two weeks?"

"So this is just a disagreement in efficiency then?" I asked.

"Something like that. At any rate, I suspect we very much have the same goal at present. You need a benefactor here in the district, and I can do that for you, but on a condition of course."

"I'm not fond of conditions."

"I want to be your partner."

"I do just fine on my own, thank you," I said. "Plus, let's just say you draw a little too much attention."

She grinned. "You sure do know how to compliment a lady, Mr. Carson."

Having a partner was something that never interested me. I'd always turned down the opportunity when it presented itself. I couldn't deny the truth though. I needed a partner right now, and this cat was probably as good as any I was liable to find at the moment. With her resources, it opened a lot of doors that would otherwise be closed. I also got the impression she was highly competent.

"I can tell just with how the conversation has gone so far that I'll not talk you out of this. Fine, partner. Mind giving me a place to stay? We can meet there in the morning."

She smiled. "There's a modest hotel not too far from here. I'll call in a reservation. It should be ready by the time you get there. Good night, partner."

40

There was no such thing as a modest hotel in Adria, or a modest anything here, really. It was just the second fanciest place I'd ever slept in instead of the first. I had breakfast and a much-needed bath. Then I waited patiently for my... new partner to arrive.

There was a knock at my door at about nine.

"Come in. Door's open."

She walked in, sporting a suit and fedora like what I was wearing when I met her the first time. How was it I kept finding myself working with comedians? Though, no one could argue she didn't make the get-up look a lot better than it did on me.

"Good morning, Mr. Carson," she said.

"Really?"

"Really, what?"

"Sugarplum, private detective?"

"That has a nice ring to it, Mr. Carson. Perhaps I'll adopt the title more officially."

"I thought you said you liked making money."

"Good one. So far I'm losing money."

"Fair enough. Here's the plan-"

"Rescue Rico?"

"How'd you know?"

"The look on your face yesterday when I mentioned he'd been caught. I did some digging last night, you might even say detective work. I think our best bet is to get into the manager's office at daddy's casino. That's where a lot of his top cats spend their downtime. They use that same office as a central point for a lot of their other work too, namely involving real estate."

"You're quick on the uptake, Sugar. Maybe I should be your partner instead," I said through a small smile.

"Oh, and that's not all. I brought the plans for the casino. Swiped 'em from daddy's office a while ago and made a copy. Figured they would come in handy one day, and now here we are."

"You really don't have a lot of trust in your dad, huh?"

"Would you?"

"Definitely not."

She went over the ground floor while showing me the stairs, fire alarms, offices, and exits. She did the same for the second floor. Looks like I could've done a lot worse with partners. I knew there was a good chance she would double-cross me sooner or later, though she seemed to be giving it straight about her dad. For now, that's all that mattered.

"Excuse me, detective. I need to get dressed more appropriately for a casino."

She went into another room, and shortly after came out wearing a sparkling ebony evening gown. It sure was strange how a dame like that could drop from the same tree as that lousy father of hers.

"What do you think?" she asked.

"I think no one will notice I'm even there. Should work out swell."

"Shall we?"

We made our way to the casino and discussed our plan on the way. We would watch the main office until the manager went on break. When he walked out, Sugar would create a small distraction. This would give me a few seconds to get up the stairs and into the room without anyone noticing. Next, I would look for anything that had to do with Rico or a possible location where he could be held. Hopefully I'd be in and out the second-floor exit before he finished. If not, I would have to rely on another, more improvised distraction.

Things went a little like that and not like that upon our arrival. She stood next to one of the tables, giving a slightly too-loud speech about how poker was the best card game. Then she gave pointers on how to bluff even the staunchest poker players. That got just enough attention from the patrons, and as such I was able to sneak up the stairs and into the office. I checked around carefully.

Eventually, I found a folder with some recent properties that were purchased at the request of Mr. B, but I heard footsteps before I could look inside. It was too late for me to get out.

"Well, hello there Nigel."

It was Sugarplum's voice, coming from just outside

the door. She'd noticed someone coming and saved my hide.

"Sugarplum? What are you doing here?" he asked, startled.

"Why, I came here to see you."

"I somehow find that hard to believe."

"Why?"

"Didn't you call me... what was it again? A 'nauseating yes-cat?'"

She giggled. "Oh, that was ages ago. Surely you are not that soft of heart."

"It was last week."

"Was it? Oh, you know how us women are. One day we want something, and the next day we change our minds."

"I wasn't born yesterday. I may not be as smart as you, but I'm smart enough to know when I'm being duped."

I finally found what I was looking for. A small storage building, leased just last month. Isolated, and not likely discovered by accident. Too small to be of any real commercial value. I waited for my chance to escape out the door and through the second-floor exit.

"All right, let's play it straight. I'm here to discuss a business proposition with you for something just over the horizon. It may benefit from someone with your expertise. Interested?" she asked.

"Let's sit down in my office."

I tensed up, looking for a place to scramble and hide if I needed to.

"No, it won't take long. Let's get a snack at the bar."

"After you," he said.

I heard their steps fade down the stairs. That was some quick thinking. Maybe this partner business wasn't such a bad idea after all.

I jetted out of the office and through the exit on the second floor.

41

I waited back at the hotel. I didn't want to take any unnecessary chances that might spoil Sugarplum's plan. She was only about fifteen minutes behind me.

"So, how did you shake Nigel Moneybags?" I asked.

"Nothing special. We concluded our conversation."

"So, what was that business proposition all about?"

She grinned. "Is that jealousy I hear in your voice?"

"Fine. Fine. Sorry I asked. Anyway, I got the goods." I invited her to sit at the table with me and I slid the folder across to her.

"Have a look. See anything interesting in there?"

She flipped through the pages until she got to the small warehouse. "That one. There. That could be the place."

"Good. Yes, I think you may be right."

"So, what's our next move?"

"Your next move is to put on that detective costume of yours, 'partner'. Ready for some field work?" I asked.

"Give me five minutes."

She wasn't kidding. She was dressed and ready to head out in three.

Even though we had an address, the warehouse was a real pain to locate. We had to go down one street, which was easy enough. Then down another street that had the name torn off the sign. We had to find a local to ask which one it was. Then, we had to walk what seemed like forever until we finally made it to a large row of identical abandoned storage buildings. I had Sugarplum scout it out once we could identify which building was ours. If she got caught, it would be a lot easier for her to talk her way out of trouble with little incident. She disappeared around the building only to come back into my sight to give me the signal to get closer. Luckily for us it was summer, so they'd propped the back door open to help with the heat.

We took a careful peek inside and realized only one cat was guarding the whole place. But the real surprise came when we saw the other occupants. There were at least a dozen dogs and cats tied up to metal poles along the wall, none of which I recognized. We waited for a while to see if anyone would show up, but no one did. Which made sense given how remote this place was, but it meant we really lucked out. Taking care of one goon would be child's play for the two of us. I asked Sugarplum to do what she did best - put on a performance. She went around to the front door and knocked loudly.

"Help! Help, I'm lost!"

As soon as he turned his attention to the front door, I rushed up from behind and gave him a hard knock in the back of the skull with my baton. I was really beginning to love this thing. We wasted no time untying everyone as soon as he hit the floor.

The first dog I untied didn't want to stick around to talk. Can't say I blamed him. I had more luck with the second one. He said they had a beagle with them until this morning. Early this morning, a few cats in suits came and took him. Only him, none of the others. They told him they had a better place in mind to host a guest of his stature. Only problem was he had no idea where they went. The trail had gone cold. Again.

We got everyone untied and sent them on their way. Any of them we could get to listen to us we asked to contact the police. Not sure how many of them would trust the police enough to do it, but just one or two would be enough. We had to let Patches know about this and quick. He may have already gotten a lead on where they moved Rick. It was the best shot we had.

I rushed to a payphone, rang up HQ, and asked dispatch to transfer me to the chief. She told me the chief had been placed on temporary leave by a judge pending investigation. I asked to be transferred over to Buddy instead, and he was in a fit. He explained that the same judge who had been prosecuting criminals fairly since Patches became chief had now flip-flopped on them overnight. He was also refusing to talk to police. Buddy asked me to pay him a visit and look into it. He suspected foul play, and I was sure he was right.

42

After I hung up the phone with Buddy, I filled in Sugarplum on the whole situation. Figuring we'd already wasted enough time, we made quick work out of heading to the Capitol District. We were both going to be out of our element now. I doubt Sugar was any better at handling the bureaucrats than I was. Maybe worse even, as hard as that might be to believe. She was quite the free spirit.

Capitol District, at least, was not a difficult place to enter. That was in part, I theorized, because it was one of the most boring places in the city. Some of the most insufferable people around inhabited it. You could get in so long as you didn't look too shady. The overall value of this place had improved dramatically in just a short amount of time. I suspected that was thanks to payments from Mr. B for services rendered.

If he wanted a law changed, it didn't take long for it to change. In their spare time, which for these jokers was all of their time, they usually sat around in the Leader Hall bickering or pretending to bicker about things and problems that didn't exist until they talked about them. You might describe them as actors. Actors for a play you would never want to go see but they still forced you to buy tickets for. You didn't just pay to see the play either. You paid to produce it, you paid for the building the play took place in, you paid the actors in the play, and for anything else they may want to waste money on. I suspect that some may disagree with me, but having lived in the Black District for as long as I have, I felt I had credibility to say it: this was the worst place in the whole city.

We made our way to the judge's house and knocked on the door. A voice shouted through the other side, but the door remained shut.

"Are you with the police?" the voice said.

I shook my head. "No sir, no police here."

"You work for the police?"

"No sir, not working for the police either. We work for you. We're here to help you with your current predicament."

The door flung open, and an old German Shepherd ushered us inside.

"What do you mean 'working for me'?"

"Just what I said. Was it extortion? Blackmail? Kidnapping? Or are you expecting a big payday? A little icing on that big fat cake of yours?" I asked.

"Sounds like you know this district pretty well, Mister..."

"Carson. This is my partner, Sugarplum."

"Now, wait just a minute. Sugarplum? That fiend's daughter? This some kind of trick?"

"No trick. Believe it or not, she's on our side. That, and we're probably your biggest allies in this whole city at the moment."

Sugarplum, who'd been quiet throughout the whole conversation, finally joined in. "What's he done that's got you switching sides so close to the end of the war?"

"I'm a judge. I'm not on any side if I'm able to do my job properly. He tried a few things, actually. First, he offered to pay me off. I should have reported it to the police, but I was afraid that might further provoke him. I should have realized that I had already provoked him by treating these cases fairly. Next, he dug up dirt on me. Sure, it might prevent me from being elected another term as a judge, but it was nothing that would get me removed from my seat immediately. I broke a few laws in my career as a lawyer. You know how that is. Occupational hazard.

"He became even more persuasive when none of that got me to budge. The police had my family hidden away, but he got to them anyway. I'm sure it's because he still has a few moles there, and not because he found them on his own, or by chance. He's keeping my wife and sons somewhere, I'm sure here in the Capitol District. He couldn't have taken them far without being noticed.

"He gave me the names of a few of his boys he needed let off and asked that I hold the new chief up temporarily. Mr. B turned himself in as all of this was being carried out and, given his prominence, they have offered him an expedited trial that is to take place just days from now. No doubt turning himself in is part of his plan and carefully timed. He knows he has little to worry about going forward, should he be found not guilty for all of these accumulated crimes.

"There are plans to pack the jury with those loyal to him, and I'm powerless to stop it. They will find him not guilty, and that verdict, as a result, will ruin the credibility of the new chief who spent night and day putting everything together. He'll get the can and we'll get another stooge for a chief. Things will be even worse than they were before. Mr. B is clever. He didn't make it to where he is now by accident. He won't make the same mistakes again."

"You mean unless we can find your family in the next couple of days and get them out," Sugar said, sounding unconvincingly optimistic.

"In time for the trial? You'd have to do so before his cronies fill the jury roster. You'd have to allow enough time for witnesses to hear about the chief being reinstated and be willing to even show up to the trial. Do you have any leads?" he asked. His face told me everything I needed to know. He had no hope.

I thought for a moment and came up with a quick plan. "I might have one."

43

I thought of an old friend of mine, Mr. Bones. Chances were good he had the information we needed. I rang up Buddy and got him caught up on the whole situation. Told him I needed to see Bones without delay. He said he would have him transferred to headquarters for a proper police interview. Because of regulations, they would allow only one officer to interrogate Bones, but luck seemed to finally be on my side. Either Patches outright forgot, or he neglected to remove my name from the official roster. The next morning I arrived at headquarters. Bones was waiting for me in an interview room, and Sugarplum had to wait outside, much to her disappointment.

I sat down across from Bones and studied his appearance closely. He didn't look well. Actually, it's not that he didn't look well. It's that he seemed to have lost that bright, indestructible confidence he had before. With good reason too, all things considered.

"You being treated all right, Colonel?"

"You know, Trigger, I'm a little smarter than I look.

Maybe not by much, but a bit. See, I don't blame you for everything that went down. I can only assume that you played a role in setting me up because you were let off. Probably a big role. Truth is, you didn't make me do anything. Me getting caught would've happened sooner or later. Now I assume that since you had me transferred here for an interview, I must have something you need." He crossed his arms and leaned back in his chair. "One thing that hasn't changed at all is that I'm in this for me. If Mr. B won't back me up or bail me out, and I don't benefit from protecting him, then any information I may or may not have is fair game. But before I tell you anything, I want assurances. *Quid pro quo* and all that."

"Fair enough," I replied. "Since you're on the level, let's play it straight. I can't promise you jack. I'm not even sure I'm still officially a cop. It's just that I forgot to quit or they forgot to take my badge. What I can tell you is that me and the new chief go way back. You tell me what I want to know, and I can all but guarantee you I can get a quarter of your sentence stripped away." I smacked the table. "Just like that."

"I suppose that's a decent starting point," Bones mumbled. "But before we settle on the cost, I want to know exactly what you're expecting that offer to buy you."

"Mr. B has a secret holding place in the Capitol District. I need to know where that is."

"I spent all my time in Adria. What makes you think I know anything about some secret safe houses in the Capitol District?"

"You're telling me you never had to transfer someone

out of that place and into Adria or transfer someone there?"

He chuckled. "Oh, Trigger. You don't know as much as you think you do."

"What's that supposed to mean?"

"This place you're talking about. Sure, some get transferred in from Adria occasionally. However, no one gets transferred out. Understand? It's the last-stop shop. The final destination, if you get my meaning. It's a long stay. Could be permanent."

"I'm not sure I understand. You wouldn't transfer someone halfway across the city just to off him in some secret location. Tell me if I'm hot or cold here. This must be the place for people who get caught up in the political side of things. Those cats and dogs in the Capitol District are a lot more ruthless. Can't have anything getting out and swaying public opinion. So where is it?"

He laughed. "I think I must be underplaying my hand a little. Judging by your interest in this place, I'm guessing valuable witnesses against Mr. B are being held there. Possibly even the family of the judge or jury members? That's exactly what it is, isn't it? Well, since we're playing for such big stakes, I still want a good deal here - even though I'm not eager to do any big favors for Mr. B anymore. For what you're asking, nothing less than dropping all charges will do."

I slammed my paws down on the table. "Drop all charges? You must be out of your mind. Have you seen the list of charges you're up against?"

He nodded. "Fair enough. Perhaps it is just a hair too much to ask."

"At the very least."

He leaned in, smiling. "Let me up the offer so you're still getting a good deal. On the big day, I'll testify against Mr. B. A lot of the witnesses won't show and you know it. I know a lot and I'll spill it all. So get the chief in here to sign off and we'll call it a day. I'll send you on your way to that secret location, and we'll all pat ourselves on the back for a job well done."

"The chief's been placed on temporary leave by a judge, for reasons you're smart enough to guess," I said.

"Look, I know you and the chief go way back. You give me your word, I'll give you the address. You take care of the judge's little problem and get the chief reinstated. Get him in here to sign the papers, and you'll get the testimony. What do you say?"

"You got a deal."

I stood up and offered my paw. He stood up and shook it, that bright expression returning. I handed him a pen and paper, and he wrote the address.

I wondered how the chief would feel about all this. He'd have done the same thing I'd wager, and there was a time I'd have resented him for it.

44

I took the address, rushing to meet Sugar out in the lobby, and we hightailed it back to the Capitol District. It turned out I had been to this house before. I'm not sure why I didn't recognize it sooner, but this was the house of my old friend; the mayor's son, Jimmy Jim. It's not that it surprised me, but he would recognize my face. We'd either have to bust in swinging and do things the hard way - with who knows how many goons to take on; or, we'd have to do this Sugar's way. I was still busted up, so the hard way wouldn't do.

Chances were that Sugarplum would be recognized too, but in her case she was counting on it. I hid around the corner to the side of his home, to give her plenty of distance. She knocked on the door and Jim answered.

"Sugar? What are you doing here?"

"What do you think I'm doing here, Jim?" she replied, a touch of venom in her voice.

He shrank back a little. Her tone indicated he should know the answer, but he was afraid to speak too quickly.

"I might know. Didn't you and your dad have a falling out?"

"Yes, and as punishment, he sent me here to see you. Can you imagine? Surely I haven't been *that* bad."

"Always the bottomless well of wisecracks, huh, Sugarplum? So, what is it you need? Everyone's here that should be here, just like he asked."

"I'm not sure what wisecracks you mean, Jimmy. My father has found you to be a... oh, how to put this nicely... an idiot. I'm sure you're aware of how important this matter is."

"An idiot? Sure, I've made mistakes but—"

"Finally, a point of agreement for you and I."

"You're a real charmer, Sugarplum. Sure, I've made mistakes, but I've always done exactly what your father asked of me," he whimpered.

"Jim, this is the single most important thing my father has ever asked you or anyone else to do. How many of my father's cats are guarding the prisoners?"

"Guarding? From what exactly? This is probably one of the most secure places in the city, just because it's one of the best hidden. Who will suspect anyone is being held in the basement at the mayor's son's house?"

"In that case, mind if I come inside Jimmy? I have business I'd like to discuss with you."

"Sure, right this way."

I waited outside for over an hour, and in that time I schemed about what I might do if she didn't come out. I wasn't really in any shape to attempt a rescue, but surely old Jimmy Jim wouldn't pose that much of a threat, even to a busted-up pooch like me. Experience told me he was as yellow and as delicate as a daffodil.

I tightened the bandages up around my ribs, pulling out my now trusty electric baton. I made my way toward the door when the sound of a turning handle stopped me. I quickly retreated to my hiding place and watched. Out walked Sugarplum, the judge's family, Brutus, and Rick looking a bit worse for wear.

There's no way it should've been that easy. I still couldn't get a read on Sugarplum. There was something likable about her, and I believed everything she'd told me. The way she shook Nigel at the casino and Jim just now left me wondering. However, I didn't have time to look a gift horse in the mouth.

I caught up with the group once they were out of sight of Jim's house, but something told me I needed to help Rick hide his identity.

"Hey, Sugarplum, how did you pull that off?"

She winked. "With persuasion, my friend. How else?"

"Could you be a little more specific?"

She shrugged. "No, I'm afraid I can't. A girl has to keep at least a few secrets."

"I'll trust you, Sugar. I really hope I don't regret this. At any rate, I've met Rico before. I don't see him here."

Rick took my cue and spoke up. "Rico? That thief everyone used to talk about? No one else has been there with us. You think it's possible he escaped on the way here?"

Sugarplum scratched her chin. "If Rico escaped, daddy would be embarrassed enough he wouldn't want anyone finding out. Considering we've never been able to catch him before, I guess he could've found what he was looking for and escaped as he was being transferred here. Sounds like he may have allowed them to capture him on purpose. Either way, it's good he got away."

I nodded, satisfied that I had obscured the situation enough to at least get her mind off of it for now. "So, we've got two key witnesses and the judge's family. Your father won't be happy when he hears about this," I pointed out.

"Oh, by the time my father hears about this, it will be far too late for that to matter."

We made our way back to police headquarters and settled everyone in. Buddy and I agreed they needed to be kept there until the big day. I rang up the judge, letting him know his family was safe. I let him speak to them on the phone, just so he would know it wasn't a trick. He immediately had Patches reinstated as chief. He wasn't thrilled with me when I told him about the deal I'd made with Bones without consulting him first, but after a lengthy and loud "discussion" we both agreed that the benefits far outweighed the cost, and he ultimately signed the paperwork dropping all charges. If Patches had taught me anything, it was the real meaning of having to break a couple of eggs to make an omelet. We were talking about a big egg in this case, but it was going to make for one satisfying omelet.

45

Finally, the big day arrived. The so-called journalists were swarming outside the courthouse. A large crowd of citizens had also gathered, which could more accurately be called an excited mob. It seemed like everyone had shown up except for most of the key witnesses. Brutus and Bones showed, at least, and I suspected Rick didn't want to come because Mr. B had discovered his identity. He was afraid of being exposed and distracting everyone from the trial.

We were all ushered inside and sat at our appropriate spots. It was clear Mr. B wasn't aware of what had been happening over the past couple of days, considering the look of surprise that came over his face when Patches walked into the courtroom wearing his badge. His surprise escalated further when he saw Brutus walk inside. When he saw me, he may as well have seen a ghost. For all intents and purposes, he had.

A different judge was presiding now since the other one was now a valuable witness. One that, sadly, also did not show. It was important to remember that things could still go south here. I had never met this judge. I could only hope that none of Mr. B's plants had wormed their way into the jury. Everything else was just for show. Everyone knew he was guilty; it was just a matter of being allowed the "privilege" to make it official.

Mr. B's lawyer repeatedly made a show of asking if so-and-so witness was present, while calling them to the stand only to feign dismay when they didn't come. As they were saying, if he was so guilty, then why did no one bother to show up to get him convicted? This went on for what felt like an eternity before he finally called Brutus forward. They swore him in and sat him on the witness stand.

Mr. B's lawyer, a slick young tabby named Rory, approached. "Mr. Brutus, tell us why you're here today."

"I'm here so I can watch that scumbag Mr. B get hauled off to jail, permanently."

Rory turned around and opened his arms to the courtroom audience before looking to the jury. "My friends, can you not hear the animosity in his voice? Mr. Brutus here thinks he's already made your decision for you. He's already decided on Mr. B's guilt; and so should you. Is that not right, Mr. Brutus?"

"I don't *think* he's guilty. I know—"

"You understand the concept of a yes or no question, don't you, Mr. Brutus?"

"I do."

"So, let me ask you again—"

The lawyer for the prosecution, an elderly dog named Gabe, raised his paw. "Objection."

The judge nodded in his direction. "Please get on with the questions, Mr. Rory."

"Thank you, Your Honor. Mr. Brutus, were you, or were you not, under the protection of a legitimate insurance policy against damage to your property or violence to your person that was supplied by my client?"

"I wouldn't call it legitimate, no."

"But why had you consistently paid for it for so long?" He turned to the jury before Brutus could answer. "After all, how many of you here would pay for a service, willingly, that you knew wasn't legitimate? And over a long period. Consider that." He turned back to Brutus, awaiting an answer.

"Because the insurance is against him and his goons. If you didn't pay it, you got a visit–"

"Mr. Brutus, can you honestly tell me you know, with no doubt, my client employed those who made threats against your business?"

"It was obvious when the threats were followed by the condition of whether I paid the insurance money."

"Mr. Brutus, is it not entirely possible that these thugs had a vendetta against my client and sought to sully his good name?"

"No, it's not possible."

"Not even in theory, Mr. Brutus?"

"Anything is possible in theory."

"So, by your own admission, it is possible then. One final question. Before today, have you ever met my client in person?"

"I haven't."

Rory frowned and looked to the jury, shaking his

head in faux disappointment. "No further questions, Your Honor."

I hated these lawyer types. I wished I was close enough to trip him on his way back to his table. *Now that would've been a sight.* I never could trust a lawyer as far as I could throw them. They only cared about getting paid, and they'd take money from anyone willing to give it to them, even the lowest of the low.

Gabe stood and walked to the witness stand.

"Mr. Brutus, I'd like to apologize to you on behalf of the city for the poor treatment you and your business have received. I'd also like to apologize for the city's failure, until today, to deliver justice to those responsible."

Rory raised his paw. "Objection, Your Honor! The defense is asking questions, not giving a speech!"

The judge nodded in agreement.

"Now will be a good time to take a thirty-minute recess. Mr. Gabe, I urge you to use that time to consider your questions more carefully. You will have an opportunity to address the court in a more general fashion in your closing statement." He banged his gavel. "The court is now in recess."

46

Once we'd all returned and resumed our positions, Gabe straightened himself and approached the bench with new confidence. "Mr. Brutus, when you opened Starlight Theater, were you approached by Vash or by those in his service?"

"I was approached by several cats in suits who represented him."

"And what was their proposal?"

"I could pay their protection fee, or I risked significant harm to my business and myself. A steep fee due monthly that could change by any amount at a moment's notice."

"And this was not a typical insurance policy, correct?" Gabe asked.

Rory stood abruptly. "Objection, Your Honor. The prosecution is leading the witness."

The judge nodded. "Sustained. Please rephrase your question, Mr. Gabe."

Gabe took a deep breath and turned back toward

Brutus. "Please describe your impression of this arrangement to the courtroom."

"What I was paying for wasn't protection from outsiders, but from them."

"And your evidence for this?"

"It was widely known and understood. If you were late, you got a visit from the ACPD in Adria who gave you less-than-polite warnings to pay up."

Gabe feigned surprise. "The police coming to collect payment for a legitimate insurance business?"

"That's right. In fact, they caught Colonel Bones doing that very thing. He was since arrested and removed from duty, along with his entire department, including the chief. They gave me a sound beating right there in my theater."

Rory stood up again. "Objection. Your Honor, none of these so-called witnesses are present here. Mr. Bones was removed from duty but hasn't stood trial yet."

The judge shook his head. "Overruled. Please continue, Mr. Gabe."

"Thank you, Your Honor." He turned back to Brutus and continued, "There was an incident in your theater involving a movie reel. Could you explain that incident to the court?"

"We'd had a movie produced that painted Mr. B in a favorable light. I showed it to a large audience, many of which were Mr. B's cats and dogs. A dog, Marty, who worked for Mr. B, replaced the reel to sabotage us. It was the same movie, but the voiceover was insulting Mr. B. It horrified us, and because of that reel Mr. B had our theater shut down until I could prove who was responsible. Fortunately, I hired a private detective who, along with the police, found the evidence in his home."

"I see. He had your theater shut down for showing a short movie clip with a voice that said bad things about him?"

"That's correct."

"Just before this trial, someone paid you a visit. You almost could not make it here today to testify. Care to explain that to the court?"

Rory stood up. "Objection. Your Honor, there is no proof that any of this ever happened. They told the police that the mayor's son was involved. The mayor's son! He denies it and has not yet been charged."

"Overruled. Mr. Rory this is your first warning. Mr. Brutus is a witness. We're all well aware that this is just his side of the story. Please continue, Mr. Gabe."

"Thank you, Your Honor," Gabe said. "Go ahead, Mr. Brutus."

Brutus nodded. "Because of what had taken place when my theater was shut down, I took it personally. I decided, based on nothing more than principle, I would no longer pay the protection money. I was ashamed that I'd paid it as long as I had, to be honest. I'd been a coward. Sure enough, the ACPD came to visit me several times, and they became less and less friendly each time. Eventually, I was given a final warning. After ignoring that one, Colonel Bones and several of his officers came to my theater. This was when they gave me a sound beating right there in front of all the critics. They were there to see a special screening that day. The beating was bad enough I had to get patched up in the hospital."

"Mr. Brutus, does this sound like the dealings of a legitimate insurance business to you?"

"It most certainly does not!"

"Mr. Brutus, you get to see many people in your line of work. The movies you've shown in your theater entertain families, adults, and children alike. Do you believe this city would be a better place without Vash?"

"I do."

"Your Honor, I have no further questions for the witness."

The judge looked over his notes before saying, "Mr. Gabe, please call the next witness."

"The prosecution calls Mr. Bones to the stand."

A series of gasps let loose around the courtroom. Expressions of shock and dismay followed. I hoped that all of this didn't backfire. We'd dropped all of Bones' charges based merely on him giving his testimony. Not necessarily that he would give it in such a way that would be harmful to Mr. B and helpful to us. We would just have to count on the fact that Bones really was in it for himself, and that he had more to gain from us than from Mr. B right now.

47

Bones was sworn in while Gabe made his way to the witness stand to begin questioning. "Mr. Bones, I trust that you've been paying close attention to the testimony of Mr. Brutus?" Gabe asked.

"I've been hanging off every word."

"Excellent, because some questions I have for you pertain to his testimony. I'm sure you understand why."

"Completely."

"Mr. Bones, can you state before the jury here today, and everyone else in this courtroom, that Brutus's testimony is true or false?"

"I can tell you that, without hesitation or reservation, all of Brutus's testimony is true, at least as it relates to me."

More gasps erupted in the courtroom; the judge banged his gavel on the stand. "I will have order in this courtroom!" The whispers and the gasps quieted, but only somewhat. The judge banged the gavel several more times until the room was silent. "Please continue questioning, Mr. Gabe."

"Mr. Bones, have you ever considered yourself a party to a legitimate insurance business?"

"No, can't say I have."

"Mr. Bones, how did the police in Adria come to work for Vash?"

"Well, the old chief is what one might refer to as a useful old idiot. As for how it all got started, that was a little before my time. However, my role as the one who ran the show in Adria was just a matter of simple compensation," Bones explained.

"Could you tell the court what you mean by compensation?"

"Everything. Fancy suits, fancy watches, fancy buildings and offices, a nice big home. You imagine it, and if you make Mr. B happy, he'll give it to you. He's very generous to those who are useful to him. Myself, until recently, for example."

"In case it wasn't clear already, please elaborate to the court as to what he expected you to do to receive this compensation."

"It was just two things. One was just as Brutus said. I'd send some of my boys to help encourage people behind on their payments to become current again. We gave several warnings, and eventually, I'd go myself. Sometimes we got a little rough."

"And the second part, Mr. Bones?"

"The second part? Well, that one was even easier. Much easier, actually. It was to do nothing."

"Nothing?"

"Exactly. If a crime was reported, and someone informed us that Mr. B was behind it, then we were expected to turn a blind eye and sit at our desks. We could do as we pleased if it was anyone else. In fact, if the crime was in direct conflict with one of Mr. B's operations, then we were expected to come down hard on it. Pile on all the charges we could come up with. Make up a few if necessary."

"Mr. Bones, would you consider any of Mr. B's operations here in the city to be legitimate? Based on your knowledge of the law and experience as an officer?"

Bones chuckled. "I had never thought of it before, but no. No, I can't really think of a single one."

"No further questions, Your Honor."

Rory bolted up from his seat so quickly that you'd almost think someone had set his pants on fire. He approached the witness stand. "Good afternoon, Mr. Bones."

Bones grunted.

"Mr. Bones, your career in Adria was that of a police colonel. Is that correct?"

"Yep."

"In that time you admit that my client was quite the benefactor for the Adria Police Department. Is that correct?"

He grinned. "You could say that."

"Yes, I could say that. I could say anything. I'm not questioning myself, Mr. Bones. I'm questioning you. Is that correct, Mr. Bones?"

Bones grinned, verging on a laugh. "That is correct."

"When you were relieved of your duty, it resulted

from a mistake you alone had made. Is this also correct?"

"Yep."

Rory turned to face the jury, expecting that some were already following where this line of questioning was going. He gave them a validating nod. "When you were being considered for removal, you were expecting my client to come to your aid, were you not?"

"It was a possibility."

"Mr. Bones, do you think it might be reasonable for some in this courtroom to suspect that, because my client didn't come to your aid, you were resentful about this?"

Gabe raised his paw. "Objection. Your Honor, Mr. Rory is venturing into the realm of hypotheticals here."

The judge nodded. "Sustained. Mr. Rory, let's avoid speculation and stick to the matter at hand. Please continue."

Rory's face twitched and his brow furrowed, and he was slow to answer. "Apologies, Your Honor." He turned back to Bones. "I'll leave you with one final question. In any of these so-called shady dealings which you had with Vash, was he ever present?"

"No, never." Bones had stopped smiling. It was another blow to their case against Mr. B. Could anyone on the jury be dumb enough to doubt the case based on something so insignificant? Yes, anything was possible, especially that. It was a real shame, but it was better to risk being at the mercy of a group of fools than one corrupt individual. This was the best chance we would ever get.

Rory walked away from the witness stand. "No further questions."

48

The judge looked through his notes. "Mr. Rory, please call the next witness to the stand."

"We call Trigger to the witness stand."

I had butterflies in my stomach. In my career, I'd sat on that witness stand many times, both as an officer and as a private detective. None of those times involved anything like this. They put a stepping stool next to the stand and a large cushion on the seat so I could see everyone, and they could see me.

"I'm a little confused. Do I address you as Lieutenant Trigger or Mr. Trigger?" Rory asked.

"Let's go with the easy one. Mr. Trigger is fine."

"Are you not an officer?"

"Technically. With all that's been going on, I haven't turned in my badge yet. You could say I had more important things to do."

"The court might find it a little strange that you can't seem to decide on whether you're an officer or a private detective."

"Is there a question in there somewhere?"

"I was just observing that it was strange is all."

Gabe knocked gently on his desk. "Objection, Your Honor. Mr. Rory is once again taking us on an involuntary adventure into the land of speculation."

The judge nodded. "Sustained."

Rory nodded, now entirely composed again. "Mr. Trigger, what exactly brought you to Adria?"

"Brutus hired me to investigate the reel swapping incident."

"And who did you discover to be the culprit?"

"A security dog by the name of Marty. We found the original reel at his residence. We believed him to be working for Mr. B."

"Purely speculation?"

"At that point, yes. Purely speculation."

Rory tensed when I said "at that point." He was quick to move on from it. "Mr. Trigger, what about the second time you found yourself in Adria?"

"Personal business."

Rory paused, thinking carefully. "No further questions, Your Honor."

Rory had played it safe. Rather than talk me into a corner, he avoided the possibility of talking himself into a corner.

Gabe approached. "Good afternoon, Mr. Trigger."

I returned a curt nod.

"Mr. Trigger, you were originally a police officer before you became a private detective, correct?"

"That's correct."

"You were removed from this position by the former

corrupt chief for what most would consider outstanding integrity as an officer. At least, that's what I've been told by several officers who worked with you. Is that also correct?"

"I'd like to think I was just doing my job," I replied.

Gabe turned to the jury, nodding to them knowingly. "How are your wounds healing?"

Rory raised his paw. "Objection. That's irrelevant. Mr. Gabe can make small talk with the witness on his own time."

The judge shook his head. "Overruled. We don't know it isn't related. Please continue, Mr. Gabe."

"Thank you, Your Honor. Please answer the question, Mr. Trigger."

"I'm still pretty beat up. According to the doctors, I should only just now be up and about. But it's nothing a little time won't heal."

"Mr. Trigger, I would like you to tell the court how it was you received those injuries."

"Oh, I'd love to. See, just days ago I got a visit from that dog I helped put away in Adria, Marty, at my office. Only, he wasn't alone. He brought a friend with him."

That big grin Mr. B kept on his face at all times was slowly, but surely shriveling away. He had been so careful never to be present during his dirtiest deeds, but he made it a point to break that rule, just for me. He must've considered the visit to be no risk at all. I was soon to be a dead dog, and dead dogs don't talk. But here I was. Talking. His curiosity to see the dog who had caused him so much trouble, in person, had killed one of the best arguments the defense had made in this trial. Curiosity killed the cat, as they say. Maybe it wouldn't kill him, but killing his chances of escaping justice was good enough for me.

"And this friend of his, would you recognize him?" Gabe asked.

"Sure, I could point him out to you right now."

"Mr. Trigger, please point out this individual to the court."

I pointed straight to Mr. B. Noise erupted in the courtroom. Mr. B himself shot up from his chair, barely able to contain his anger. The judge banged his gavel repeatedly. "Order! Order!" Several individuals, many who I know must've been plants, had to be dragged out. Many of them screamed about how I was a liar, or how Mr. B had helped them with such and such and blah blah blah. As for Mr. B, his lapse in composure was only momentary. Though still not smiling, he sat back down quickly before anyone else had even noticed. Then he was calm again.

Gabe made his way back to the witness stand. "And you're certain it was Mr. Vash in your office?"

"Absolutely certain."

"Did Mr. Vash say anything?"

"He ordered Marty to make quick work of me. I'm sure it was the only reason he bothered to show up. Dead dogs don't talk. He introduced himself before he left. Then Marty gave me a good thrashing, which led to my office being burned down. I got lucky and by some miracle fought him off. I escaped the building before the whole thing went up in smoke."

Gabe turned to the jury. "So much for never being there himself and always blaming it on someone else. No further questions."

Everyone was on edge since the outburst. You got the feeling that everything seemed to go our way, but no one dared to get their hopes up. We still had one wild card to overcome: the jury.

The judge shuffled through his notes. "After a short recess, we'll return for closing statements."

49

Gabe was the first to make his closing statement. He wobbled about on his cane, but with his shoulders firmly back and his head held high.

"Dogs and cats of the jury. Many brave dogs and cats worked tirelessly to bring us together on this auspicious day. Some paid with their lives or their livelihoods. They all gave something so you could inherit a safer city. A safer city for your kittens and puppies, for your wives and for your husbands. For your grandchildren and their grandchildren. And not just a safer city either, but one that is more prosperous."

Gabe continued, "Imagine how much these businesses might grow without the constant threat of thugs breathing down their neck, making threats, and stealing money from the hungry mouths of their workers. Sure, this may not be as much of a problem in Adria, but look at places like the Black District. Mr. Vash's despicable behavior has smothered out the desire of the young people there and all over the city. Why bother opening a shop when you're just going to be harassed and bullied? Why be honest when it's crime that pays? Our youngest citizens, our children, who would otherwise take up honest trades when they grow up, are being groomed by gangsters and thieves. Now, I'm not naive enough to believe that this problem will be gone completely, but you... it is in your power to deal it a serious blow today."

I thought back on Clive and how he and his family might be doing. He was just the sort of lad Gabe was describing. Undoubtedly many of these jury members knew someone like that. Maybe they'd even been someone like that. Maybe they were someone like that now, planted there by Mr. B for a verdict of not guilty. My attention snapped back to Gabe's statement.

"I also want to give a message to those of a particular purpose among you. Yes, we know you're here, but no, we don't know who you are. I'm speaking to those who were planted here by Mr. B to ensure that, yet again, he gets off without so much as a slap on the wrist. Consider breaking ranks. Consider casting away whatever payment he promised you. Do something far more valuable for yourself. Maybe you've been promised treasure. Sure, he will make good on his payment. We've already heard here today that he rewards those who serve him well, but consider for a moment a different reward. You may struggle tomorrow without his more direct reward, and the next day, but over time you will suffer less and less. Most of all, you will save your city and the lives of your neighbors, your friends, your family. Is that not the greater reward? I only ask that you consider it carefully. That is all."

The judge himself appeared moved by the speech. He took a moment to gather his composure, doing his best to appear impartial. "Mr. Rory, your closing statement please."

"Thank you, Your Honor."

Rory walked the length of the jury box, his energy and youthful vigor spilling out into the air itself.

"People of Arc City. Members of the jury. What has Arc City ever done for you? My client is just one cat in a city of thousands of cats and dogs. Could all your misfortune really be blamed on this villain, Mr. B, Vash, even if he was as terrible as the prosecution has told you he is? Could there even be such a boogeyman? Let's all think about this question and be reasonable. There cannot be.

"I'm sure many of you can remember when Adria was not such a productive and prosperous place as it is now. Yes, there's more crime, but there's also more of everything. More wealth, more entertainment, and more opportunity, for everyone. I'm sure many of you have heard of or frequented many of my client's businesses. He has donated real money to your schools and police forces. He has employed hundreds. He's also the reason Mr. Gabe and myself can now stand before you as equals, both attorneys, both respected by this court. I'm sure many of you remember a time when I wouldn't have been allowed such a privilege, simply on the basis of my species. You'll not find another in the city more dedicated to the advancement of the civil rights of cats. Vash has brought real progress to this city, and this... this is how he is thanked.

"As for these bullied business owners experiencing

buyer's remorse with their supposedly terrible business insurance? We have put together statistics showing that nearly every business owner who duly paid their premiums operated almost entirely without incident. If you ask me, that's money well spent.

"If you convict my client today, consider what the city will be losing. Is he really the legendary villain you have all come to fear, or is he merely a convenient scapegoat for the incompetence of your police and leaders? Don't let yourself be told what to think by all the so-called evidence. Think for yourselves. That is all."

I knew what Rory had been saying was littered with nonsense, but I couldn't help feeling that part of it was true. That old chicken-and-the-egg question. Was Mr. B just a symptom of a broken system, with corrupt leaders looking for a payoff? Corrupt police giving in to the first thug to make them a nice offer? Patches had shown us, through the recent accomplishments of the police, that things could've been different all along. We now had a straight-laced cop heading the ACPD, and we arrived here in no time. Mr. B couldn't be entirely to blame for that, could he? In the end, it didn't matter. He'd done what he'd done, and he needed to face justice for it. We'd bring the others to justice tomorrow, setting an example for them to fear today.

Nothing was ever as simple as just one cat or one dog. No problem was so small that getting rid of one cat or one dog would fix it. But whatever happened, we'd be ready for it.

The jury was dismissed and deliberated for only an hour before returning. A young cat girl handed the judge a small envelope and took her seat. Mr. B smiled and nodded at her. I knew exactly what that nod meant.

"Vash, please stand and receive the jury's verdict," the judge demanded.

He complied, standing confidently behind a podium facing the judge, his smile never fading. The judge opened the envelope at what seemed like a snail's pace. After reading over the letter calmly and carefully, he addressed the courtroom.

"In the case of Arc City versus Vash, and regarding all charges presented, the jury finds Vash, otherwise known as Mr. B... guilty of all charges. As allowed by law, I am delivering the maximum sentence, life in prison, with no chance of parole. Vash, let me just say it gives me great pleasure to send you to prison for the rest of your life. You will never see the light of day again as a free cat."

Vash just continued smiling. "If you say so, Your Honor. I'll see all of you again very soon."

He said the words as if, beyond all doubt, he knew them to be true. As for whether or not I believed them, I suppose anything was possible. If he'd already made arrangements, it would be difficult to discover them. If I had to guess, though, it was just wishful thinking on his part. He assumed this would be just another problem for him to buy or threaten his way out of, but he was wrong. This was the end of the line for Mr. B.

50

The city quickly erupted with celebration and riots alike, those two groups clashing with one another as the news spread. It would die down in a few days, and we'd get to see how the dust settled. I made my way to Adria to pay a visit to a cat I knew would be sympathetic to those celebrating. She's probably having a celebration of her own.

I made a stop by Rick's office before I went to see her. He'd heard the news on the radio and was apparently waiting for me. He had two glasses sitting on his desk with an unopened bottle beside them. He poured both to full and slid one across the second I walked in.

"We did it, detective. We did it," Rick said, taking a sip.

I was taken aback by the fact that there were no jokes or jests from the usually goofy beagle today.

I hung my head. "You deserve more credit than me. I would've been content sitting in that office scraping by for the rest of my days. The city had given up on me, and I'd given up on it. I'd convinced myself I couldn't make a difference, even if that's what I wanted. Worse still, I convinced myself that I didn't want to make a difference. You, on the other hand—"

Rick motioned for me not to continue. "I had the means. That's the only difference. I have no higher character than you. I'd argue less, actually. If I'd been the one sitting in that office in Black District, I'd have been too much of a coward to take all the physical risks you did. I'm fortunate enough to have the wealth and success I do to give me other options, though I worked hard for it. Still, there's a big serving of luck involved as well." His smile grew wide. "Speaking of which, I thought it had run out recently. Thank you for rescuing me. There's no way I was getting out of there alive."

I chuckled. "Don't mention it. I didn't find out they kidnapped you until after I already made it back here. I tried to find you to come up with a plan. I ran into Sugarplum after I found out you weren't here. We... by the way, did you ever look into this Bad Kitty character?"

"No, I'm afraid I didn't have the chance. Would you still like me to?"

I pondered the question for a long while. "I'm not sure she's even an enemy. Let's leave her alone for now."

"If you say so."

We spent the next several hours chatting and looking back on events. I told him about my plans to use the money from the last job to open a new office in the Black District. He talked about how he'd gotten caught on purpose to help the judge's family but found himself unable to escape. We shared a laugh about it. When I realized how long I'd been there, I stood up and offered my paw. We shook and I left the office. A private detective becoming good friends with one of the most wanted criminals in Arc City history. How's that for irony?

I went to see Sugarplum, who promptly showed me to her new office. It was modest for her and standard fare for a business office, but still a nice start.

"What do you think, Trigger?" she asked, eager for an answer.

"Elaborate for a private detective's office. We could spend a few hours pouring dust around here and there while throwing papers on the floor to make it more authentic."

She put her paw over her mouth to stifle her laughter. "Oh dear, no. I think I'll turn my father's cover business into a real business. Insurance in the form of private security. We'll staff your business with trained security personnel. For a fee, of course, but we'll cover the expenses if anything happens to your business. What do you think?"

"I like it better than beating people up if they don't pay you money. I think this is even legal, too. A big plus."

"Trigger, you've helped me a great deal—"

"Yeah, see to it I don't regret that," I grunted.

"No promises," she said. "What can I get for you? Name one thing. Anything. I'll get it for you. Name it and it'll be yours."

"Anything at all?"

She nodded in confirmation. "Anything at all."

I left the building, a content smile across my face, giving my pocket a triumphant pat.

My next stop was Blue District headquarters. I walked into Patches' office where he was joined by Lieutenant

Buddy and Lieutenant Petey. Except Lieutenant Buddy was now Colonel Buddy. Patches assigned him to head up the Adria division, charged with cleaning up both the division and Adria itself. It was quite the job and a responsibility that no one envied. I slapped Buddy on the back and offered him my congratulations.

He shook my paw. "Why don't you come join me in Adria, Trigger? Just keep that old badge in your paw there and forget you ever came to give it back."

I smiled back at him. I'll admit that the thought crossed my mind. I got a little choked up when I tried to answer.

Patches spoke up and saved me the embarrassment. "All right ladies, I need to see the big hero here. Why don't you catch the rookies up on your plan for the coming weeks?"

The two nodded at each other, with Petey making imitation punches toward me as he walked out, laughing. Nothing could bring these dogs down. They were in quite the mood.

Patches closed the door to his office as he said, "You thought about it for a minute there, didn't you?"

"I did."

I placed the badge in Patches' paw.

He shook it in the air, smiling. "This is yours, any time you want to come back and get it. You'll always have a place here."

"It's good to know there are still honest cops I can call if I get into trouble. Some folks will still be afraid to go to the police, but they'll come to me. The city needs someone like that. So long, Patches. I'll be seeing you around." We shook paws, and I headed toward the door but stopped short. "Oh, one more thing." I reached into my other pocket, pulling out the gold watch Mr. B had sent me and gently tossed it onto the desk. "Auction that thing off. It ought to fetch enough to outfit every officer in the Black District with those fancy zap sticks they have in Adria."

"Where did you... Nope, never mind. I don't want to know. Thank you, Trigger. See you around."

I left and headed toward my final stop of the day, a payphone just outside my old office. I rang up Lily and asked her to meet me on the bench just across the street from what was left of it. After she left me have a word in, that is. She did think I was dead for a time, so it was understandable that I'd get an earful.

While I waited, I took the opportunity to rummage through the debris. I'm not sure what I was hoping to find, but I didn't find it. It's amazing how hard it is to recognize what things are after they've been burned. In a way, it wasn't just my office that ended up this way. It was hard to look at any part of my life from before Lily walked in with her missing collar problem, and see myself as the same dog.

When I saw Lily approaching, I walked across the street and sat on the bench. She sat down beside me, silently looking over the burnt rubble.

"Are you going to open a new office somewhere?" she asked.

"Right there, actually. Going to purchase the lot from my old landlord and have a new building built there. The landlord's actually an architect. Maybe I'll have him design the new one."

"I look forward to seeing it," she said, pausing for a moment before continuing. "I heard about what happened. You're getting a reputation as quite the hero around here. I rather admire you, and your courage, detective."

"It's funny, Lily. Now that I think about it, it's your case that got all this started, and how it all ended."

"How it all ended?"

I picked up the small box sitting at my side and handed it over to her. "Here, this is for you."

"Shall I open it?"

I nodded. She opened the box and dropped it onto the ground below, placing both her paws over her mouth, her eyes welling up with tears.

"You found it! You really found my mother's collar."

I grinned and scratched the back of my head, not prepared for the surge of excitement. She lunged toward me and hugged me tightly.

"Oh, Trigger, even if you weren't anyone else's hero, you'd still be mine."

Maybe this job wasn't so bad after all.

EPILOGUE

"I can do this," Constance whispered to herself.

This was the moment she had been waiting for her whole life. A chance to finally claw her way out of the Black District slums, and into a life of glamour and fortune in Adria. She'd finally be able to wear the latest fashion, enjoy the finest dining, and buy the most expensive baubles and trinkets.

No more bullying from her older siblings. No more disappointment from her mother. No more judgmental glances from passersby. No more stealing to pay the rent for an apartment no one should even have to stay in for free. No more sobbing into her pillow at night, waiting for a handsome rescuer who would never come.

"I just have to deliver one message, and it's home free. Big payday here I come!" She still whispered, but her excitement was getting the better of her... just a bit.

She was told it would be dangerous, but there was no danger as far as she could see. The dark streets of Arc City might be scary for a cat like the one who hired her, but not for her. She'd grown up on these streets. She could feel when she was being followed. She could sense eyes on her. She knew which back alleys were safe, and which where a death sentence. She wasn't a big cat, but her claws were sharp, and she'd used them before. Good enough to win a lot of fights, but more than good enough to run away from the ones she couldn't.

"This must be it," she said, letting out a huge sigh of relief as she arrived at the entrance of an old, rundown apartment complex. "This dog's apartment isn't much better than mine. Wonder what's so special about him?" Then she realized it wasn't her job to wonder about it. It was her job to follow the instructions in the letter and be on her way. She was just the go-between, and that was fine by her.

The front was locked, but she'd never met a side entrance she couldn't quietly sneak into, so that's what she did. In this case, the best option was a fire exit on the second floor down a side alley. She ran toward the opposite wall, jumped and kicked off, and caught the bottom of a raised ladder on the opposite side. As she pulled herself up, she was startled by a shift in the moonlight she'd noticed out of the corner of her eye and snapped her attention to the roof of the opposite building.

She hadn't made a sound, and no one had been following her, as far as she was aware. She scanned her surroundings for a few minutes, but nothing presented itself. There was a light wind and the smell of a coming rain creeping into the night air. Probably a stray piece of litter blowing by. No one was that stealthy, so it must have been. She gathered herself and wedged open the door, entering the dark hallways of the apartment's shared interior space.

She was in luck. Only a short distance down the hall was the door she'd been looking for. In just a few short hours, she'd be back in Adria, this time to stay. Then, it would be on to the next job, and a new life. She took a deep breath, raised her paw, and prepared to knock on the door. Before she could bring her paw forward, she noticed a line of vertical light land on the door, and slowly become smaller as it travelled along the wall back toward the fire exit. The fire exit!

She looked up, just in time to see it close quietly, leaving the interior nearly pitch dark again. Her cat eyes adjusted quickly, and although she couldn't see perfectly, she could see a figure slowly moving toward her in the dark. She wasn't alone.

DID YOU ENJOY THE BOOK?

If you did, please consider leaving an honest review over on Amazon. As an independent author, reviews are critical in helping me reach more readers like you, and your feedback helps me to improve. I love hearing what you have to say, and I read every one.

Oh, and I've got a little something for you...

FREE BOOK

A never before told story of Arc City's most powerful crime boss. Get ready to have everything you thought you knew about Mr. B turned upside down as you discover his true origins. He may be the most infamous criminal in Arc City history, but he wasn't born that way. Follow him on his journey from the oppressive Black District slums, to the luxurious Adria District penthouses, and every triumph in between.

Get your copy here:
MAOwens.com/FREE

CONTINUE THE SERIES

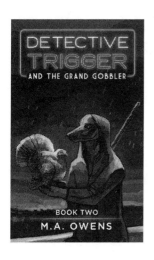

Trigger, the Chihuahua private detective, needs a little R&R. But, no sooner does his retreat begin before he's pulled into a new case — one with an eerie connection to his last one. This time, though, things take a disturbing turn — the would-be client is murdered!

Now, Trigger is hot on the trail of the most dangerous foe he's ever faced. If he doesn't unravel the mystery quickly, he may find himself the next target of the brazen killer.

Can he solve the case before the murderer strikes again?

Get it here:
MAOwens.com/TheGrandGobbler

SOME OTHER WAYS TO FOLLOW

Amazon
amazon.com/author/maowens

Bookbub
bookbub.com/authors/m-a-owens

Email
info@maowens.com

Facebook
fb.me/maowensbooks

Goodreads
goodreads.com/maowens

Newsletter
(if you got the free book, you're already on it)
maowens.com/newsletter

Made in the USA
Columbia, SC
16 October 2020